Nancy,

from

Grandma.

Hope the chicken Pocks
are better.

" BUY A BRACELET ?" SHE ASKED.

Honey Bunch : Her First Auto Tour.   *Frontispiece—(Page* 123**)**

HONEY BUNCH:
HER FIRST AUTO TOUR

BY
HELEN LOUISE THORNDYKE
AUTHOR OF "HONEY BUNCH: JUST A LITTLE GIRL,"
"HONEY BUNCH: HER FIRST DAYS
IN CAMP," ETC.

ILLUSTRATED BY
WALTER S. ROGERS

NEW YORK
GROSSET & DUNLAP
PUBLISHERS

Made in the United States of America

CONTENTS

CHAPTER   PAGE

    I   PENNIES TO SPEND   1

   II   TRYING THE NEW CAR   13

  III   DADDY MORTON'S PLAN   25

   IV   A PARTY PICNIC   38

    V   A NEW KIND OF UNCLE   50

   VI   THE ROYAL GREEN AND BLUE TOUR .   61

  VII   SOME PRESENTS   73

 VIII   SOMETHING SAD HAPPENS   85

   IX   TIME TO START   96

    X   HONEY BUNCH AND STUB   108

   XI   THE GYPSIES   120

  XII   AUTO CAMPING OUT   133

 XIII   THE SPARE WHEEL   146

  XIV   THROUGH THE WOODS   159

   XV   HOME AGAIN   172

HONEY BUNCH:
HER FIRST AUTO TOUR

CHAPTER I

PENNIES TO SPEND

"And she fell off the porch backward, in the rocking cha~ ~~ ~ded on her head right on the si~ ~ ~aid Honey Bunch.

Ida Camp shook her head solemnly and then remembered what her Great-aunt Martha sometimes said.

"Tut! Tut!" sighed Ida, clicking her small red tongue sadly. "Tut! Tut!"

"Right on the sidewalk—smash!" Honey Bunch repeated.

"Was she killed and everything?" asked a voice which apparently came through a crack in the fence. "Say, Honey Bunch, was she killed?"

"That's Norman," Honey Bunch whispered to Ida.

The two little girls stared at the fence which began to behave very queerly. It shook and rattled and it seemed as though some one was pounding on the other side of it. But presently, with a last tremendous rattle, the cause of all this noise was explained—a small boy hoisted himself up and scrambled into place so that he was sitting on the top of the fence with both legs dangling on the side that faced the yard where Honey Bunch and Ida were.

"Was she killed?" he asked again.

This was Norman Clark. Mrs. Miller, who came to wash for the Mortons, called him "the fence boy." Mrs. Miller said Norman ought to grow up and be a carpenter and build fences to climb on.

Honey Bunch liked him. She liked all the children in her neighborhood, and she was used to answering Norman's questions.

"Was who killed?" she asked patiently now.

"The lady who fell off the porch backward in a rocking chair smash on the sidewalk," Norman replied, proving that he must have listened carefully through the crack.

Honey Bunch looked at Ida Camp. They both giggled.

"It was Anna's doll—Anna Martin's doll," explained Honey Bunch. "She left her out on the porch of their house and the thunderstorm yesterday afternoon tipped the chair over."

"Huh—all that fuss over a doll!" Norman said gruffly.

He was much put out to discover that he had been interested in a conversation that had to do with dolls and he lost no time in hurrying on to things that were more suitable for boys.

"I'll bet I know something you don't know," he said mysteriously, kicking his heels against the fence so that it swayed.

Every spring Norman's father and Honey Bunch's father put new supports in the fence, so that it wouldn't come down with Norman.

"I know where you're going," said Norman, staring hard at Ida.

Honey Bunch turned her yellow head quickly and looked at Norman. Then she laughed softly, a dear little laugh that sounded as though she must have a pleasant secret all to herself.

"He means where we are going this afternoon, Ida," Honey Bunch said.

Then Ida laughed, too, and Norman began to frown.

"I don't see anything funny," he said crossly. "I'll bet you don't know how I found out where you are going."

Honey Bunch was too polite to tell him, but Ida didn't mind. She was usually a very shy little girl and liked to hide behind Honey Bunch when they went anywhere where there were strange people. But Ida knew Norman Clark and she was not at all afraid of him.

"You listened," said Ida calmly. "You listened through the hole in the fence. But you can't have any, because only girls are going."

"Honey Bunch," Norman looked at the little girl as though he might be going to cry in another minute, "didn't I give you some of my licorice shoe strings the last time? Almost a whole string, didn't I?"

"Yes, you did," replied Honey Bunch, nodding her head. "Ida, he'll have to come with us. There's Kitty and Cora now. Come on—it's all right, Norman, if you want to come."

Norman slid down from the fence and trailed after the girls. He knew they were going to the candy shop to spend ten cents—ten cents apiece. He had heard them talking about it earlier in the afternoon. And for ten cents you could get some of the best candy in Miss Roxie's little store. All the mothers in Barham allowed their children to buy candy from Miss Roxie—she made it all herself and it was, as Honey Bunch had once told her daddy, "just too pure for anything."

It is odd how news spreads. By the time Honey Bunch and Ida and Kitty and Cora Williams and Norman had reached the corner, Mary and Fannie Graham and Anna Martin had seen them from the porches of their houses and they came running out to go with them. On the next block there were Teddy Gray and Lester Fox and Paul Niles playing hop scotch, and of course they asked Norman where he was going and of course Honey Bunch invited them to go to the candy store.

"My land! How many do you think can get in here all at once?" asked Miss Roxie in her high, cracked voice when she came out to see who was ringing the bell on her door.

Miss Roxie's shop was a little square room and it opened on a wide porch that had no roof over it—it was more like a platform than a porch. When any one opened the door of the shop a little bell jangled and then Miss Roxie came in from the kitchen where she was making candy, to see what was wanted.

Eleven children crowded into that one small room filled it pretty full, and as they all began to say at once what they liked, no wonder Miss Roxie was bewildered. But she knew what to do. Miss Roxie was used to children and she was really very good to them. She

never made them hurry when they were trying to choose what kind of candy they wanted
most, and she would even take back one kind
and give another, if the bag was handed back
to her before she went back to her kitchen.

"Who has the money?" said Miss Roxie
wisely.

"Honey Bunch and Ida Camp," Norman
announced. "They each have ten cents to
spend."

"Then let them spend it," said Miss Roxie.
"Stand back—Honey Bunch is so little you'll
push her over the counter if you are not careful."

"I think it would be nice," Honey Bunch
declared, staring blissfully at the red gum-
drops, "for every one to buy a cent's worth of
favorite candy. Ten cents is enough, isn't it,
Miss Roxie?"

Miss Roxie hastily counted the bobbing
black and yellow and brown heads.

"There won't be any for you," she said.

"Oh, but I have ten cents," Ida cried anxiously. "Let every one have two cents' worth

of favorite candy. That will be nicer yet."

But Miss Roxie said she had some molasses cooking on the stove and she positively could not wait while they chose so many different kinds of candy.

"Anyway, my arithmetic can't do so much long division," she told the children. "You each pick out five kinds, Honey Bunch and Ida, and I will put it in two separate bags and then you can settle it with your friends when you get out on the street."

It was very hard to choose five kinds of candy when there were eight kinds in the glass case and all were beautiful, but finally Honey Bunch and Ida did it and found themselves with two bags of candy. Then the children trooped outside and Miss Roxie went back to her candy making.

"Let's sit down here and rest," suggested Cora Williams, dropping down on the top step of the wide porch built around the shop.

They all settled down in a long row and Honey Bunch passed her candy bag first.

"I can't stay so very long," she said, trying not to watch Norman anxiously as he put his fingers in—one never knew what would happen to a candy bag when Norman held it.

"I have to go home pretty soon," went on Honey Bunch, sighing with relief when Norman passed the bag to Teddy Gray.

"Why?" Anna Martin asked curiously. "Did your mother tell you not to stay?"

"No. But I think it is most time for Daddy to come," said Honey Bunch.

Ida Camp nearly swallowed a marshmallow, she was so eager to talk.

"Is he going to bring the car?" she asked.

Then she flushed scarlet as Honey Bunch looked at her reproachfully.

"I—I forgot," stammered poor Ida, and the tears came into her eyes.

"Car!" Norman shouted. "A new car, Honey Bunch? What kind is it? Where is it? Can I go around the block in it?"

"My mother said to wait till Daddy brought it home and then you could all come to see it," explained Honey Bunch. "But Ida forgot not to tell. Don't you care, Ida—Daddy won't mind."

"Take the cinnamon stick," Ida urged. That was her favorite candy. "Take it, Honey Bunch—I'm so sorry I forgot."

She started her candy bag down the hungry line and Honey Bunch, to please her, took half the cinnamon stick.

"Is it a new car, Honey Bunch?" Teddy Gray questioned eagerly. "Is it bigger than the old one?"

"I don't know. But it is different," said Honey Bunch. "This is a touring automobile motor car."

Lester Fox laughed, but the other children were much impressed.

"What is a touring automobile car?" Paul Niles wanted to know.

"I know!" cried Cora Williams. "My Uncle Richard has one! He goes to Canada every year on a hunting trip. It's just like a camp, with a stove and beds and a tent and everything."

Honey Bunch pulled a tiny embroidered

handkerchief from the pocket of her pink linen dress.

"Yes, that is the kind it is," she said positively. "Mother said there is an ice box and a stove so we can cook right outdoors."

"Oh—oh—Honey Bunch!" gasped all the little girls together. "Cook right outdoors without a chimney? You never can!"

"My mother says so," Honey Bunch repeated.

"Well, if your mother says so, I suppose you can," said Fannie Graham. "But I should think the smoke would choke you," she added.

"The candy's used up," Norman pointed out. "And perhaps if we go back Mr. Morton will be there with the car. I'd like to see the tent."

But first Norman had to blow up one empty bag and make a terrible noise by dashing it against his palm. Then Teddy Gray had to blow up the other, and as he closed his eyes to blow he couldn't see Paul Niles, who crept up to him and broke the bag before Teddy was ready. They made so much noise that

Miss Roxie came out to see if any one was hurt and she was surprised to find they were "only fooling."

"I thought you were stepping on each other," she said, peering at them over her round spectacles. "Well, have a good time—you're only young once."

When the boys had finished with the empty candy bags, they all hurried back to Grove Street where Honey Bunch lived. Norman was a little ahead, and as he turned the corner he began to wave his arms like a windmill.

"It's there!" he screamed. "Come on! It's there!"

He began to run, and all the children ran after him. Loud and hoarse, as they ran, they heard the noise of an automobile horn.

"Honk! Honk! Honk-k!" it called to them cheerfully.

CHAPTER II

TRYING THE NEW CAR

"YOU wait, Norman Clark!" called Cora Williams angrily. "You wait for Honey Bunch. I guess it is her car!"

Honey Bunch was running as fast as she could, but she couldn't run as fast as Norman did. But Norman waited till she caught up with him, and they all reached the shining new automobile, drawn up at the curb before the Morton house, at the same time.

"Hello!" said Mr. Morton. "I began to think the neighborhood was deserted."

Mr. Morton was Honey Bunch's daddy, and he was quite the nicest daddy in all the world. Honey Bunch was sure of that.

"Take us all for a ride, Daddy?" Honey Bunch asked, patting the square tin box on the shining new running board affectionately. "Please, Daddy?"

"Could we go?" teased Norman, his eyes

trying to see all the things at once. "Say, it is a dandy car, isn't it? There's the tent and look at the stove! And a trunk in back and everything!"

The children stared at the car, and two or three people who were walking by stopped, too.

"New car, Mr. Morton?" called Mrs. Farriday from her parlor window.

She lived next-door to Honey Bunch, and of course she was interested in what they did and where they went.

"You've bought a new car, haven't you, Mr. Morton?" Mrs. Perkins called, from *her* front window.

The Perkins' family lived on the other side of the Morton house.

Daddy Morton laughed, but before he could say anything the front door of his own house opened and Mrs. Miller came down the steps.

"I thought I'd just come out and see the new car a minute while my starch is cooking," said Mrs. Miller.

Mrs. Miller was the washerwoman, and she was one of Honey Bunch's best friends. The little girl was very glad Mrs. Miller had come to see the new car and she began at once to show her all the " 'tachments," as Anna Martin persisted in calling the tent and the stove and the ice box.

"I guess I know!" said Anna, when Norman tried to tell her she was wrong. "I guess I know! My mother has a new sewing machine and all the things that go on it are 'tachments. So there!"

"Gee, I never saw a car with so many things before," whispered Paul Niles to Teddy Gray. "I'd like to ride in it."

Daddy Morton overheard him and smiled.

"After a bit, perhaps, Paul," he said kindly. "I've heard that all things come to children who wait patiently. I want to take a little run out into the country with Honey Bunch and her mother first. Ah, here comes Mrs. Morton now."

Honey Bunch's pretty mother ran down the steps and seemed surprised to find such a large group standing around the car. Mr. Morton got out and helped her in, put Honey Bunch on her lap, and then took his place at the wheel again.

"Stand back a little," he cautioned. "Mrs. Miller, hang on to Norman or he will be under the wheels. We'll not be gone long. Good-bye, everybody!"

The long, shining car shot up the street, while Honey Bunch tried to wave to Mrs. Miller and the boys and girls standing beside her and to Mrs. Farriday and Mrs. Perkins.

"I hope Mrs. Perkins saw me," she remarked, as they turned into a small park." "Once I hurt her feelings when she didn't see me waving."

Of course, Honey Bunch was not the real name of this sunny-faced little girl sitting on her mother's lap in the new automobile. Dear no! Honey Bunch had a much longer name, though she seldom heard it. Gertrude Marion Morton—that was her "serious name," as Mrs. Miller had once said. But she was so little and so sweet and her eyes were so blue

and her hair was so yellow that her daddy
declared there was just one name that really
suited her. That was "Honey Bunch," and he
began to call her that when she was a little
baby, too small to walk. Then her mother
called her Honey Bunch and the aunts and
uncles and cousins took it up, and presently
the little girl almost forgot her longer name.
In the first book about her, which is called
"Honey Bunch: Just a Little Girl," it has been
explained that no one could say "Bunch of
Sweetness" every time they spoke to her, even
though that was what she was. Her daddy
said so. "Honey Bunch" was easier to say.

Well, Honey Bunch was such a little girl
that every day was a new experience, and she
had wonderful times, whether she was help-
ing Mrs. Miller, or visiting her cousins in
New York, or other cousins who lived on a
farm. Honey Bunch planted a garden, too,
and raised prize-winning flowers the very first
time she tried it.

Then she went camping with her daddy and
mother, and the exciting things she did and

saw there are described in the last book about her which is, "Honey Bunch: Her First Days in Camp." Honey Bunch made many new friends in camp and she hoped that some day she might go again to Camp Tickaloc.

Now she was at home again and there was a secret to think about. Honey Bunch was wondering about this secret as her daddy drove the new car through the little city park and out on the highway that led to the open country. For Honey Bunch knew that this "automobile touring motor car" was to take them all on a trip, but she didn't know where the trip was to be!

"Around the world, Daddy?" Honey Bunch had whispered, when she first heard that she was to go traveling.

"Oh, my, no!" Daddy Morton had answered, pretending to be shocked. "We couldn't go around the world, because Daddy couldn't spare the time. Nearer home than that, Honey Bunch."

"Down town," said Honey Bunch wisely,

and her daddy had laughed and pulled her down on the couch for a pillow fight.

But that had been three days ago, and here was the new car and still Honey Bunch did not know where they were going.

"Daddy?" she asked softly. "Daddy dear, perhaps it is time now to tell about the secret."

"My secret?" said Daddy Morton, making his eyes very large and round as Honey Bunch did when she was trying not to tell something. "Why, Honey Bunch!"

Honey Bunch leaned over and rubbed her yellow head against his shoulder.

"I wouldn't tell any one but Ida and Kitty and Cora and perhaps Anna," she told him coaxingly.

"You're a wheedler," said Daddy Morton, turning the car into a dirt road, bordered on either side by scrubby little bushes. "But wheedle away, because I am not going to tell just yet. I like to have a secret."

"Do you know, Mother?" Honey Bunch asked quickly.

Mrs. Morton kissed her and said, yes, she knew, but she liked a secret, too.

"You and Ida Camp have dozens of secrets, Honey Bunch," said Mrs. Morton. "So Daddy and I thought we would have one. You shall know by and by—it isn't really settled yet. And, David, doesn't it look like a storm to you?"

Mr. Morton glanced at the sky. When they had started the sun was out, but now the sky was a dull gray.

"Wind's changed," said Honey Bunch's daddy. "I don't think it will rain, but I don't like to take a chance. Perhaps we'd better turn. I can't risk heating the engine."

"Don't let the new car get wet," begged Honey Bunch earnestly. "I like it all new and shiny, Daddy. Don't let it rain on it, please."

"Well, Daughter, I'll do my best to get back to the garage before it does rain," Mr. Morton promised. "You like everything clean and shiny and unscratched, don't you, dear?"

"Yes, I do," replied Honey Bunch. "Mrs. Miller says that neatness is a virtue."

Daddy Morton threw back his head and laughed so loudly that a cow looked over the fence at him in great surprise.

"You and Mrs. Miller must have some great talks, Honey Bunch," said her daddy, when he could stop laughing. "I know she misses you when you are away."

"I miss her, too," Honey Bunch answered.

It looked as though it were surely going to rain any moment, and other cars were hurrying to get home before the drops fell. Some automobiles shot past Daddy Morton so fast that they made Honey Bunch blink her eyes and made Mrs. Morton fear they might be crowded into the ditch.

"Hello, there is some one who was crowded too far," said Mr. Morton, as they came in sight of a little crowd of people standing at one side of the road.

Honey Bunch looked eagerly and saw a car tilted so that only one side of it showed from the road.

"Oh, my!" she cried softly. "I hope it didn't spill anybody."

"We all hope so. No, every one is all right," Mr. Morton said, as he saw some men fasten a towline to the car. "Just ditched. Lucky it wasn't anything worse."

They had to wait while the car was pulled out of the ditch, and then it was seen that it was not damaged except for a bent mudguard. There was room at the side for cars to pass in single file, and while the people who had been in the ditched car and the people who had helped pull them out were still talking and writing down their names in little books, the automobiles began to go past very slowly and carefully.

"Oh, Mother!" cried Honey Bunch, as her daddy drove the car past the crowd slowly. "Mother, look, look!"

"What is it, dear? I don't see anything," Mrs. Morton replied. "What is it, Honey Bunch?"

"A rabbit!" said Honey Bunch. "He's

hurt! I saw a rabbit! The car fell on him. Daddy, please stop and tell the people they hurt a rabbit."

Mr. Morton, of course, had been watching the road and he had seen nothing. Although Mrs. Morton had not seen it, either, Honey Bunch was so unhappy at the thought of a rabbit lying hurt in the ditch, she urged her husband to stop the car and go back and look.

"Ask them not to leave the poor creature there in pain," said Mrs. Morton, who was almost as unhappy as Honey Bunch at the thought of a poor little rabbit being hurt. "Do hurry, David."

Mr. Morton drove the car to one side of the road and got out. Honey Bunch leaned out and watched him walk back to where the crowd of people and two automobiles were still waiting.

"Mother, he's bringing it back!" she cried excitedly. "Oh, Mother, perhaps it can be mended!"

"Brought you something, Honey Bunch,"

called her daddy, before he reached the car. "Here is something for a little girl with sharp eyes."

He held out something toward her and Honey Bunch stared.

"It *is* a rabbit, isn't it?" she asked doubtfully.

Well, it was a rabbit, but not the kind Honey Bunch had thought at first. This was a toy rabbit—a large, stuffed rabbit, made of silver gray velvet. But he was all spotted and mashed now, because even a toy rabbit can not fall into a ditch and have a car fall on him and not show signs of what he has suffered.

"But why did you bring it to Honey Bunch?" Mrs. Morton said, holding the little pink hand of Honey Bunch firmly in hers so that she could not touch the muddy rabbit.

"Because it is a lost rabbit," was Mr. Morton's answer to this. "I thought Honey Bunch might like to give a lost rabbit a home."

CHAPTER III

DADDY MORTON'S PLAN

"I'M sure I heard thunder," said Mrs. Morton anxiously. "Do hurry, David."

Mr. Morton put the rabbit in the back of the car and took his place at the wheel again.

"I *knew* I saw a rabbit," murmured Honey Bunch, as the car sped on.

"Of course you did, sweetheart," her daddy assured her. "Not a live rabbit, though, but a big, make-believe rabbit. And some one I know has the brightest blue eyes of any little girl in Barham, or she would never have noticed."

"But whose rabbit is it?" puzzled Honey Bunch. "How did it get in the ditch?"

"Didn't it belong to the people whose car was ditched?" Mrs. Morton asked, as much surprised as Honey Bunch was.

"No one knows whose rabbit it is or how

long it had been in the ditch," Daddy Morton told them. "None of the people in the car had ever seen it before. But it is so wet and dirty and so very, very flat—the car must have fallen squarely on it—that I judge it has been in the ditch for several days."

"I saw the long ears," explained Honey Bunch, "so I knew it was a rabbit. I can have it to play with, can't I, Daddy?"

"I don't believe it is good for anything," Mrs. Morton said, glancing back at the poor rabbit lying on the floor of the car.

"Well, we'll let Mrs. Miller scrub him and perhaps he'll need new stuffing in spots and a little sewing; but, with some small repairs, I'd say he will be a rather handsome rabbit," declared Mr. Morton.

There came a little sprinkle of rain, but they were on the street where the garage was now and in another moment the car rolled safely in the door.

"Now the car won't get wet," said Honey Bunch, with satisfaction.

"We were just in time," her daddy replied,

as they heard a gust of rain tinkle against the windows. "Want to see our new kitchen, Honey Bunch?"

Honey Bunch did, and so did Mother. They had had no time to examine the new car, and here in the light, dry garage was a splendid chance, for no eager or curious neighbors would come to interrupt them. The garage was a block and a half away from the house, and no other car was kept in it.

"See, here are the pots and pans," said Mr. Morton, opening the tin box on the running board.

It was really a small cabinet, and Honey Bunch and her mother thought the kettles and frying-pans and the tin plates and cups all hung on little hooks, just like "doll things." There was the stove too, and the white ice box which Mr. Morton said would carry enough food for four days. There was a tent which fastened on to one side of the car and made the most comfortable little house to sleep in. Honey Bunch wanted to come and sleep that night in the garage with the tent in place, but her daddy was sure it would be too warm.

"Wait till we get out into the country," he said. "Then we'll have real fun. Well, I think the rain is stopping now. Who wants to run for the house?"

Then Honey Bunch took hold of Mother's hand and gave her other hand to her daddy and he took the rabbit he had found in the ditch and, after he had locked the garage doors, they ran down the street and never stopped till they came to their own house.

"Did you get wet?" asked Mrs. Miller, hurrying to the door to let them in before Mr. Morton could get out his key. "Don't tell me you got that beautiful new car all wet the first time you took it out!"

"We didn't—we didn't," Honey Bunch cried in great glee. "Daddy turned around and we came back to the garage. And I saw the frying-pans and the tent and we have a new rabbit, Mrs. Miller."

"My good-ness!" said Mrs. Miller. "A rabbit! What won't you be bringing home next?"

Honey Bunch had often tried, but she could never say "my good-ness" the way Mrs. Miller did, making two words of it. She practised, did Honey Bunch, but she either said, "my good good-ness," or something else went wrong and people were sure to laugh at her.

"A rabbit now!" went on Mrs. Miller, who was always interested in anything that happened to the Morton family. She had known them for years and years, ever since Honey Bunch was a tiny baby. "Is it alive?" Mrs. Miller asked quickly.

For answer Mr. Morton held up the rabbit and Honey Bunch couldn't help laughing. It was really a sad-looking rabbit, but it was funny, too, for some of the stuffing had been lost and it was fat in places and thin in others and so spotted with mud that it reminded Honey Bunch of the leopard in her animal book.

Mrs. Miller knew what to do at once. She smiled at Mrs. Morton and took the poor velvet rabbit into her apron.

"I'll wash him," she said, starting for the cellar stairs.

"When he is dry, I'll pad him out and mend him," Mrs. Morton promised. "Then Honey Bunch shall give him a name."

"We'll let him be our mascot when we go to—oop!" cried Daddy Morton, clapping his hand over his mouth.

"You almost told, Daddy," Honey Bunch said sadly. "In another minute you would have said where we are going, but you didn't quite."

"A minute is a great help," declared her daddy cheerfully. "You can tell a secret in a minute, or you can stop from telling it in a minute. Sixty seconds, Honey Bunch, mean that you have sixty chances to tell a secret or not to and—"

"David, stop teasing that child," said Honey Bunch's mother. "I thought you were going to tell her about the party."

Now, if there was one word that was almost as exciting to Honey Bunch as the word "secret," it was that word "party." She liked

parties, and she and Ida Camp had a birthday
party apiece every year.

"Where's the party, Daddy?" asked Honey
Bunch eagerly, forgetting all about the secret.
"Where's the party? Are we going?"

Mrs. Miller laughed and disappeared down
the cellar stairs to the laundry where she went
to work to scrub the rabbit and make him as
clean as soap and water could, which was very
clean indeed. Mrs. Morton went upstairs to
take off her hat, and Honey Bunch and her
daddy sat down in one big chair, as they
usually did when they had something important to talk over.

"I thought perhaps you'd like to give a
party before we go away," said Daddy Morton. "Your little friends want to see the new
car, and Mother and I think if we had a picnic, say day after to-morrow, and took them
all out to the country and put up the tent and
cooked on the stove and let them see just what
we are going to do on our trip, they would
enjoy it. What do you think, Honey Bunch?"

"Daddy dear!" she cried happily. "Daddy

dear, I think that is the nicest party I ever heard of. Nicer than a birthday party or when Kitty Williams' aunt took us to the movies. Can Norman come, and Kitty and Anna and Ida and Teddy—and everybody, Daddy?"

"Well, remember the car holds only so many," her daddy said, smiling. "But I think we can take all the children you know best. Count them on your fingers for me, Honey Bunch."

Honey Bunch could count nicely on her fingers, and though Norman Clark told her that when she went to school she would have to use a paper and a pencil, Honey Bunch was really learning arithmetic ahead of school time. Now she counted aloud, bending down a little pointed finger for each name.

"There's Ida Camp," counted Honey Bunch, "and Kitty and Cora Williams, and Norman, of course, and Teddy Gray and Paul Niles and Lester Fox and Albert Barnes, and Mary and Fannie Graham and Grace Winters

and Anna Martin and— How many is that,
Daddy?"

"A dozen," said Mr. Morton. "And a little
girl named Honey Bunch makes thirteen.
I'm afraid we can't take them all, dear."

"Well," Honey Bunch replied cheerfully,
"Albert is away and so is Elmer Gray—I forgot him. And Anna Martin and Grace Winters are going to the seashore to-morrow."

Mr. Morton laughed and said that would
make a difference.

"I suppose we can manage to pack in ten
children," he said. "The boys can ride on the
roof, if there is no other place. Mother will
telephone their mothers, dear; but if you want
to ask them, too, that will be all right. Just
say we are going out into the country for a
picnic supper Wednesday and would like
them to come with us."

Honey Bunch was so delighted at the
thought of this party that she went out to the
backyard at once and told Norman Clark.
He was sitting on the back fence, talking to

Mrs. Miller, who was hanging up the rabbit to dry. The rain had stopped and the sun was shining again and Mrs. Miller said she wanted that rabbit to "start drying that night."

"In the new car?" said Norman, when he heard what Honey Bunch had to tell him. "Gee, that will be fun! Does anybody know? Care if I tell the fellows? What time are we going? Do you suppose your mother will let me cook? Are we going to stay all night and sleep in the tent, Honey Bunch?"

Mrs. Miller put her hands over her ears— and very funny they looked, with a bunch of clothespins in each hand—but Honey Bunch did not mind Norman's habit of asking questions.

"I don't think we'll stay all night—there isn't room in the tent," she said seriously. "But we are going to use the stove—Daddy said so."

"I'm going now and tell Paul Niles," Norman declared, apparently falling off the fence backward.

"There, that will be a fine rabbit, with a

stitch here and there," said Mrs. Miller, stepping back to get a good look at the velvet rabbit now dangling by his long ears from the clotheslines.

He was a very large rabbit, and Honey Bunch began to be glad she had seen him. She didn't know what name to give him, and when she asked Mrs. Miller's advice, that good woman told her to "wait awhile."

"It will come to you all in a flash," said Mrs. Miller, wiping her hands on her apron and picking up the bag of clothespins. "All in a flash, Honey Bunch, and then you'll have a name to be proud of."

That night at dinner, when Daddy Morton asked her if she had thought of a name for their mascot rabbit, Honey Bunch shook her yellow head.

"I am waiting for a flash," she declared earnestly. "Mrs. Miller says a good name will come like that."

"I think after our party, you'll find it easier to think of a name," said Mrs. Morton, laughing a little.

Grove Street—most of Honey Bunch's small friends lived on the same street she did —didn't talk of much else but this "party" all the next day. The boys and girls were so eager to examine the new car and, most wonderful of all, to ride in it and see the tent and the stove and all the things Honey Bunch had told them were folded away under the seats and in boxes, that if there had not been a lock on the garage doors, it is to be feared some small fingers might have gone poking about without waiting for an invitation. But the "day after to-morrow" finally came, and that afternoon found every child invited lined up on the curb before the Morton house long before one o'clock, when they were to start.

"Here comes the car!" cried Norman Clark, who knew Honey Bunch and her daddy had gone to the garage after it, for he had seen them go.

"What's that on the front seat?" Kitty Williams asked, staring.

Honey Bunch was on the front seat beside her daddy, but Kitty knew Honey Bunch and she was not staring at her, but at something Honey Bunch held on her lap.

"A rabbit!" Norman shouted, as the car drew in to the curb. "A big rabbit! It isn't real, is it? Where did you get it, Honey Bunch? Is it yours? What's its name?"

Honey Bunch beamed upon her guests and held out the gray velvet rabbit for them to see. He had dried beautifully, and Mrs. Miller had ironed him carefully, and Honey Bunch's mother had put new cotton in him and sewed him up and he was as handsome as he had ever been. Mrs. Miller said she was sure of it.

"We found him in the ditch," explained Honey Bunch. "He hasn't any name yet. I am waiting for a flash."

CHAPTER IV

A PARTY PICNIC

MRS. MORTON came down the steps and Mrs. Miller came after her with several boxes that looked exactly like picnic boxes. You know how they look. Mr. Morton put the boxes away under the seats and then began to tuck the children in, but not under the seats, you may be sure. Honey Bunch hopped out and said that Ida Camp must ride on the front seat, and as there was room for two, Kitty Williams sat beside her. The others, with Mrs. Morton and Honey Bunch, were settled in the back, then, with only one or two little waits—once when Paul Niles dropped his knife out of the car and once when Mary Graham thought she hadn't a clean handkerchief (though she found it later in her pocket) —they were off.

The children were almost as interested in

the new rabbit as they were in the new car. It was his size that made him so much admired. He was half as tall as Honey Bunch, and when she held him on her lap, she could hardly be seen behind him.

"Daddy said he could be our mascot when we go touring," said Honey Bunch, as Fannie Graham stroked one of the long gray velvet ears.

"Where are you going?" Teddy Gray asked quickly.

"That's a secret, Teddy," said Mr. Morton, without turning his head. "Can't tell you till later."

"Oh!" Teddy murmured. "I didn't know. Doesn't any one know?"

"Not for certain," said Mr. Morton mysteriously. "But you'll hear as soon as the right time comes. What was that?"

They had just passed one of the small roadside stands where candy and popcorn and soda water and such things were on sale, and now some one was calling to them from the little booth.

"Hey, Mister!" a boy was shouting. "Hey, Mister!"

"Now what do you suppose he wants?" Mr. Morton asked aloud, but really speaking to himself, for of course no one in the car knew what the boy wanted.

"I'll run back, Mr. Morton," Norman Clark offered. "Don't back up—I'll ask him what he wants."

And before Honey Bunch's daddy could open the door, Norman had crawled over it and was running down the road.

All the children poked their heads out and watched for Norman to come back. In a moment or two they saw him, running as fast as he could.

"The poor child won't have any breath left," said Mrs. Morton, and indeed when the scarlet-faced Norman reached the car, he was panting so hard that he couldn't speak for several seconds.

"They want to know if you are going past the four cross roads," reported Norman, when he could really talk.

"Why, I suppose so," Mr. Morton said. "I hadn't thought much about it, but we can keep on this road just as well. Why?"

"Gee, I never asked him!" answered Norman. "But I will—wait a minute!" and he dashed off again.

"David, back down to the stand," said Honey Bunch's mother. "Norman will wear himself out. You can find out what is wanted much better if you ask."

Honey Bunch thought so, too, and she was glad when the long shining car backed swiftly down to the refreshment stand.

"He wants to go to the four cross roads," said Norman, pointing to the boy who had shouted after them.

"The car is pretty full," Mr. Morton declared, smiling. "But if you think you can stand on the running board and not fall off— Could you?"

"Yes, sir," said the boy promptly.

Norman and Lester and Paul and Teddy at once wanted to stand on the running board, too, but Mr. Morton would not hear of it.

"Don't you see this boy wears long trousers?" he asked them. "Well, then, when you're old enough for that, perhaps you may ride on the running board, but not now."

"I didn't mean to make you come back. I thought you weren't going to stop," said the boy. "I'm going home to get my mascot. I forgot him this morning."

Honey Bunch sat up so suddenly she bumped her head on Fannie Graham's chin.

" 'Scuse me, Fannie," she apologized.

"This is a mascot," said Norman, pointing to the rabbit Honey Bunch held on her lap.

"That's a nice one," the boy said approvingly. "Mine's a poll parrot. My brother sent him to me from South America."

"A live polly?" asked Honey Bunch.

And Norman wanted to know if he could talk.

"Here we are at the crossroads," Mr. Morton said suddenly.

"I live right through there," said the boy, pointing with one hand, while with the other he held out something to Mrs. Morton. "I'm

ever so much obliged for the lift. That's just
something for your picnic, ma'am," he called
over his shoulder as he dropped off the running board and ran toward a small yellow
house standing close to the road.

"Go on, David, don't stop," said Honey
Bunch's mother, in a queer voice.

Honey Bunch twisted around to see what
the boy had left, and even Mr. Morton
glanced over his shoulder, while the boys
and girls stared at the bottle with curious
eyes.

"Is it to eat, Mother?" asked Honey Bunch.

"He's made a mistake," Mrs. Morton said,
trying not to laugh. "He is a very nice, polite
boy, and he wanted to give us something, because Daddy gave him a ride. But the poor
child must have picked up the first bottle he
put his hands on, and he's given us furniture
polish."

Honey Bunch looked puzzled, but her
daddy said probably the boy thought he had
brought mustard or salad dressing, or something like that.

"Give it to Mrs. Miller—she likes to polish things," said Honey Bunch.

So the bottle of furniture polish was put away to be saved for Mrs. Miller, and presently the car had turned into a green lane that led to a white gate.

"We're going to show you how to camp out," said Mr. Morton. "Who wants to open the gate?"

Norman and Teddy and Paul all rushed at once, and when the gate was unfastened and Mr. Morton had driven through, they hooked it again and took their places in the car and rode down the narrow road, just wide enough for one car, for another mile or two. They were on the private grounds of a large estate, and the man who owned the place was a friend of Honey Bunch's daddy and had said they might "camp out" in his grove of trees.

"What a lovely forest!" said Kitty Williams, when they came in sight of the trees.

"Those are woods," Norman corrected her.

"Well, I guess a forest is a wood," said Kitty indignantly.

There was a wide clear space of grass just outside the woods, and Mr. Morton stopped the car here. Every one tumbled out and Mrs. Morton opened a box. Inside it were ten little envelopes.

"You remember about the children who dropped bread crumbs as they walked, so they could find their way home again, don't you?" she asked them. "Well, in these envelopes is confetti, a different color for each boy and girl. Scatter it as you walk and when it is all gone, turn at once and come back. Supper will be almost ready by that time."

Honey Bunch had blue and she scattered the tiny paper bits very carefully. She tried to "make it last." When Norman heard her say this, he at once thought of a great scheme. He wouldn't use any of his till he had found the other end of the grove. He walked on ahead and Honey Bunch lost sight of him, but Kitty Williams scattered her confetti so thickly that before she had gone half a yard she had none left.

"You'll have to go back. Mrs. Morton said

to turn around as soon as you had used up your confetti," Mary Graham called to her.

"Pick some up and use it again," advised Paul Niles, and Kitty thought that was excellent advice.

In fact, that is what they all did as soon as they had scattered their confetti. And it was such slow work to pick up the tiny pieces of paper that Honey Bunch's daddy, when he came after them to call them to supper, found most of them very near the entrance to the grove, busily trying to scrape up the little colored scraps.

"Where are Norman and Honey Bunch?" asked Mr. Morton quickly.

"I saw them just a minute ago," Paul answered. "Honey Bunch was making her confetti last and Norman was saving his."

Mr. Morton laughed and went on to look, while the others tagged after him. He was a little ahead and when they heard his shout of laughter, they began to run pell-mell, eager to see what the joke was.

There was Honey Bunch, flushed and very

much in earnest, trying to hop from one piece of confetti to another and Norman putting down a piece for her and then going back to take up the piece she had just left.

"I don't see how you planned to get home at that rate," said Mr. Morton, picking up Honey Bunch and putting her on his shoulder. "Mother wanted the confetti to bring you back to the car, you know."

"Oh, I didn't think of that," Norman admitted, looking a little surprised. "I was trying to see how far we could go."

However, of course no one was lost, with Honey Bunch's daddy to look after them, and when they came in sight of the car there was the tent in place and a frying-pan on the little stove. Mrs. Morton waved a long-handled fork at them and called "Supper!" just as though she always cooked out of doors.

The boys wanted to see how the tent "worked" and the girls were eager to examine the stove, and it is one of the nicest things about a picnic supper that you may eat and talk and go around exploring at the same time.

They had bacon sandwiches and they could take one in one hand and eat it as they looked at the tent or hung over the little stove or peered into the ice box, where, this afternoon, there was not only a lump of ice, but bottles of milk and two hard bricks of ice cream.

"Wouldn't it be nice if we could all go touring?" sighed Fannie Graham.

"I guess Mrs. Morton wouldn't want ten children with her all the time," Ida Camp said soberly.

"Here comes an extra one," said Honey Bunch's daddy. "Have we any ice cream left, Mother?"

"There's four of them in the tent," Honey Bunch announced clearly.

"Four in the tent!" said Honey Bunch's daddy. "Four *more?*"

When he looked in the tent, sure enough, there were four more children. The one Daddy Morton had seen standing off a little way, made five.

"How did you get in here?" he asked them,

as they scrambled out and lined up before the tent.

"Under the automobile," the tallest child explained, and indeed their clothes looked as though they had crawled under the car. Dirt and grass stains spattered the frocks of the two little girls and the blue shirts of the two little boys.

"Did you come to the picnic?" asked Honey Bunch.

"Yes'm," all the children said cheerfully, and the boy who had stood a little way off came nearer.

"Is that your brother?" Norman Clark demanded, pointing to him.

"He's our uncle," said the younger of the two girls.

CHAPTER V

HONEY BUNCH and her friends stared in surprise. They had never seen an uncle like this. Teddy Gray put into words what they were all thinking.

"He can't be an uncle," Teddy protested. "He's wearing short pants!"

"I am too an uncle," said the boy, rather indignantly. "There's a baby at home, and I'm an uncle to him, too."

Daddy Morton and Honey Bunch's mother had been busy cutting the half brick of ice cream that had been left after every one had had one piece. Now Daddy Morton said that if the newcomers would sit down on the grass he would give them each a plate of cream.

"I don't think the uncle should have any," Norman announced firmly. "If he is an uncle, he is grown up, and grown-up people

50

should let the children have the ice cream."

The boy who said he was an uncle looked anxiously at Honey Bunch, who had started toward him with a plate of ice cream. Mrs. Morton laughed and began to open a fresh box of little cakes.

"Give the uncle his ice cream, Honey Bunch," said her mother cheerfully. "And, Norman, you may pass the cakes. Every one is to have a cake."

"Even the uncle," Mr. Morton added, and he laughed, too.

Honey Bunch couldn't help staring at the boy, and so did her friends. They were sure there was some mistake, for uncles just had to be grown up.

"I never heard of a little aunt," said Ida Camp thoughtfully, as she ate her cake.

"Edith, this uncle business is going to be the end of us," Mr. Morton cried hastily. "I think it is time we thought about going home."

"We're going after the cows," said one of the little girls. "Do you want us to help you wash the dishes first?"

"No, thank you, dear," Mrs. Morton replied, taking the saucers and spoons they brought her. "We'll take the dishes home with us and wash them there."

The five strange children lingered to watch as the tent was taken down and the stove put back in place and everything packed away nicely.

"Don't you ever wash your dishes?" the younger girl asked Honey Bunch.

"Why, of course we do! Three times a day!" said Honey Bunch, much shocked at such a question.

"When we are touring, we'll wash the dishes after every meal," Mrs. Morton explained. "We are going right home now, and it will be easier to wash them there this time, for we won't have to wait to heat the water."

When everything and every one was in the car—and this time Norman Clark and Teddy Gray were allowed to ride on the front seat with Mr. Morton—Norman whispered to Honey Bunch.

"Ask him what his name is—the uncle one," he urged her.

Honey Bunch couldn't think of asking an uncle his name like that, but she leaned out of the car and whispered to one of the little girls standing near.

"What is the name of your uncle?" whispered Honey Bunch.

"Lysander," the little girl said loudly.

"Good-bye, Uncle Lysander," Norman called politely.

And every one of the children, as Mr. Morton started the car, leaned out to wave and shout, "Good-bye, Uncle Lysander!"

The other children waved, too, and "Uncle Lysander" swung his battered straw hat. They were glad they had come to the picnic— you could tell that by the way they smiled.

Mr. Morton laughed till he had to get out his handkerchief and wipe his eyes, but Honey Bunch didn't see anything funny, nor did her friends. And the first thing Norman Clark said when his mother asked him if he had had a good time was:

"My, yes, Mother. And what do you think? We saw an uncle with short pants!"

Honey Bunch carried in her velvet bunny and the bottle of furniture polish, and when Mrs. Miller came the next morning to wash she gave her the bottle. Mrs. Miller said she was very glad to get it, because she had been wanting to polish her music cabinet for a long time, and this would be exactly the kind of polish to use.

Mrs. Miller wanted to hear all about the picnic and so did Lady Clare. That was Honey Bunch's beautiful cat, and, strange to say, Lady Clare didn't like the rabbit at all. She knocked him down off the chair when she saw him and she even tried to chew one of his long velvet ears. But Lady Clare was very sweet and purry, when, the rabbit out of sight, she could sit comfortably on the little rug before the laundry stove and listen to Honey Bunch tell Mrs. Miller about the picnic and the uncle in short pants and the boy who had given them the furniture polish.

Honey Bunch, of course, was getting ready to go away. Her mother was very busy, and so was she. There is always a great deal to be done when you get ready for a trip, and Honey Bunch had to see that her large family of dolls had their clothes in perfect order.

"Of course I'm not going to take them all," she explained to Mrs. Miller. "I think I'll take three—maybe. But I have to leave enough clean clothes for the rest to wear while I am away."

"To be sure," said Mrs. Miller, pulling out a bit of lace on one of Honey Bunch's own pretty dresses before she dropped it into the basket. "And I'll come over once or twice a week and see that they take their baths and put on clean dresses. You know children are careless if there isn't some one around to remind them."

"Yes, I'm afraid they are," Honey Bunch agreed. "And, Mrs. Miller, I wish you'd see that they don't get their clothes mixed. Some-

times they quarrel, and I have to be just as—
as——"

"You have to put your foot down," suggested Mrs. Miller.

Honey Bunch looked at her small patent leather slipper and lifted it up a little way, then put her foot down firmly.

"Yes, I have to put my foot down," she agreed. "Children are a great care and—and everything."

"They'll be all right—don't you worry a mite," said Mrs. Miller, who certainly looked as though she never worried over anything. "I suppose Lady Clare will come and live with me while you are gone?"

"Sh—Mrs. Miller. She likes to have me tell her first," Honey Bunch whispered, looking to see if Lady Clare had overheard.

But the black cat was still asleep and Honey Bunch sighed in relief.

Mrs. Miller stirred the starch with a long-handled stick.

"Have you named your rabbit yet, Honey Bunch?" she asked curiously.

Honey Bunch shook her head and put a pair of doll's stockings into the tiny clothes basket that was her very own.

"I haven't had a flash, Mrs. Miller," she said earnestly.

Mrs. Miller laughed and just then Honey Bunch heard her mother calling.

"That means your lunch is ready," said Mrs. Miller. "Do you want me to hang out your wash for you, Honey Bunch, or shall I leave the things in the basket till you can do it yourself?"

"Oh, I want to hang them out when you do," Honey Bunch declared. "You won't hang out clothes till after lunch will you, Mrs. Miller?"

And Mrs. Miller, who had a basket of clothes ready for the line but who would do anything at all that Honey Bunch asked of her, said she would wait.

"I can be washing some of the colored clothes, just as well as not," said the good-natured washerwoman. "You run along, Honey Bunch, and this afternoon we'll put

out a wash that will make the neighbors look
twice."

Honey Bunch ran up the stairs and found
that her daddy had come home. He seldom
came home to lunch, and she was glad to
see him. She was seated at the table and ready
to eat her luncheon before she noticed that
there was a long gray letter lying beside his
plate.

"Honey Bunch, do you feel like hearing
something interesting?" her daddy asked
teasingly.

Honey Bunch's blue eyes stared at the letter.
She was sure the something interesting would
come out of that long envelope.

"I thought perhaps you'd like to know
where we are going on our trip," said Mr.
Morton, his own eyes twinkling.

"Oh, yes!" Honey Bunch cried, trying not
to bounce, because that isn't polite at the table,
you know. "I would just love to know where
we're going, Daddy."

"Well," said her daddy, picking up the long
envelope and taking a closely written letter

from it, "I've just heard that the way is open for us to take the Royal Green and Blue Tour."

Honey Bunch looked across the table at her mother.

"Is it a nice tour, Mother?" she asked politely.

"Yes indeed it is, darling," said Mrs. Morton.

"See, Honey Bunch, I'll draw you a little map," Daddy Morton began, picking up his fork and glancing mischievously at Honey Bunch's mother.

"David!" said Mrs. Morton sternly. "Daddy David Morton, I am surprised at you! Don't you know how wrong it is to draw maps on the tablecloth with a fork?"

Honey Bunch giggled and her daddy put down the fork.

"That's so," he murmured. "I almost forgot. You mustn't draw maps on the tablecloth. Remember that, Honey Bunch Morton. I'll draw a map for you on the back of the envelope—that will do just as well."

He took a pencil from his pocket and while
Honey Bunch forgot to eat her salad, she was
so interested, he drew a map of the Royal
Green and Blue Tour on the back of the long
envelope.

"We go up in this direction," said Daddy
Morton, "up, up, to the green fields of a farm
at the top of the state. Then we branch over
here and presently we come to blue water.
I'll draw a circle, and that will represent
Triplets, or the Three Lakes, as people have
named them. But we have to climb mountains
before we come to the Three Lakes."

Honey Bunch folded her napkin neatly and
slipped down from her chair, first murmur-
ing, "Excuse me," to Mother.

"I know what makes it a Green and Blue
Tour, Daddy," she said excitedly. "I have
to go and tell the other children now."

And away she dashed, forgetting all about
the clean clothes she was to hang out on the
line with Mrs. Miller's wash.

CHAPTER VI

THE ROYAL GREEN AND BLUE TOUR

"OH-HOO, Ida!" called Honey Bunch, dancing up and down on the front steps.

"Oh-hoo, Honey Bunch!" came Ida's voice, and a little figure came tumbling out of the front door of the Camp house and dashed across the street.

"Ida, we're going on the Royal Green and Blue Tour!" cried Honey Bunch, not waiting for Ida to reach the steps.

Ida did not know what the Royal Green and Blue Tour was at all, and as far as she was concerned, it might be a trip to Europe. But she saw that Honey Bunch was excited and pleased, so she was sure she had pleasant news to tell.

"How lovely!" said Ida heartily. "Then it isn't a secret now?"

"My, no!" Honey Bunch assured her.

61

"Daddy drew me a map of it. We go to green fields and blue waters and it is just wonderful."

"Blue waters?" asked Ida, puzzled.

"Lakes," Honey Bunch explained. "The Twin Lakes, people call them. No, that isn't right."

Ida sat down on the steps to get her breath.

"There are three lakes Daddy said," went on Honey Bunch. "The Triplets—that's it, Ida. Triplet Lakes. And we're going over mountains and everything."

"Are you going to take any dolls?" asked Ida.

"Eleanor and the rabbit," Honey Bunch replied. "I wish I could think of a name for him, Ida. Can't you have a flash?"

Ida shook her head. Apparently she was quite sure that she would never have a flash.

"Let's go and tell the Graham girls where you are going," she suggested.

Honey Bunch was willing, and she and Ida went to find Mary and Fannie Graham to tell them that the tour was no longer a secret. But

Fannie and Mary had gone to spend the day
with an aunt, and as she and Ida came down
the steps of the Graham house, Honey Bunch
suddenly remembered Mrs. Miller and the
basket of clothes.

"I promised to hang them out when she
hung her clothes out!" said Honey Bunch.
"Oh, my, she will think I forgot all about it!"

"I'll come and help you," Ida declared, and
they ran all the way back to Honey Bunch's
house.

Mrs. Miller had just finished her own
lunch, and she said that Honey Bunch had
come in the "nick of time" to hang out the
clothes.

"Here are some clothespins, Ida," said
Honey Bunch, proudly handing her chum
some of her own clothespins which her daddy
had brought her and which were exactly the
right size for dolls' clothes.

Honey Bunch and Ida carried the basket
of doll clothes out into the yard and Mrs.
Miller followed them with the larger basket.
Honey Bunch had a clothesline all her own,

too, and it was hung low so that she could reach it easily.

"Lady Clare looks pretty on the fence, doesn't she?" said Ida, as the black cat stretched lazily and yawned.

"Lady Clare looks pretty anywhere," Honey Bunch said. "But she doesn't like the rabbit. I don't know why it is, but she doesn't. She bit him."

"I don't think cats like rabbits," decided Ida, busily hanging up a doll's petticoat as she saw Mrs. Miller put one of Honey Bunch's petticoats on the line and pin it carefully by the waist band.

"Is this good drying weather, Mrs. Miller?" asked Honey Bunch anxiously.

"Couldn't be better. Well, I thought something was missing," Mrs. Miller said, with such a sudden change in her voice that both Honey Bunch and Ida turned to stare at her.

There sat Norman Clark on the fence and Lady Clare was walking off in the opposite direction, looking ruffled. Lady Clare and Norman were both fond of the fence, and each

had the idea that the other should keep off.
Norman didn't actually tease Lady Clare, but
he did shake the fence when he climbed up on
it, and no kitty cat likes to sit on a fence that
wobbles and shakes.

"Norman, we're going on the Royal Green
and Blue Tour!" said Honey Bunch smilingly.

"Is it very far?" Norman asked. "When
are you going? Will you sleep out in the tent
every night? Do you know how to go?"

Mrs. Miller said, "My land sakes!" and
picked up her basket.

"I'm going in," she announced. "I'll let
you know when the clothes are dry enough to
take down, Honey Bunch."

Norman sat on the fence and banged his
heels comfortably against the boards.

"We're going to green fields and blue
waters," said Honey Bunch, sitting down on
the grass, facing him. Ida sat down on the
grass, too.

"That makes it the green and blue tour,
Norman. And I'm going to take Eleanor and

the rabbit and we're going to have a lovely time."

"You always have a lovely time," said Norman, a little enviously. "How far away are you going, Honey Bunch?"

"I'll draw you a map," Honey Bunch offered. "Daddy drew one for me. Only I haven't any pencil and paper."

"I'll come over and you can get it," said Norman, dropping down to the ground.

Honey Bunch ran into the house to get a pencil and paper, and there in the hall stood Kitty and Cora Williams, who had just come to see her.

"Honey Bunch is out in the yard," Mrs. Morton was saying. "Why, no, here she is. What is it, dear?"

"I have to draw a map for Norman Clark," said Honey Bunch. "Please, Mother, may I have a pencil and a piece of paper?"

"A map?" asked Kitty Williams, as Mrs. Morton opened her desk to search for a pencil. "Can you draw maps, Honey Bunch?"

"This is the Royal Green and Blue Tour map," Honey Bunch announced. "We're going—Daddy said so. Come on out and I'll show you where we're going."

Out in the yard Norman and Ida and Kitty and Cora knelt in a circle while Honey Bunch, using a brick for a table, drew her map.

"We go away up—up to the top of the state," she explained, trying to remember what her daddy had told her. "And then we branch off like this and go to Trip-Triplets. They're three lakes and the water is blue. And we cross mountains to get there."

"But you're going down," objected Norman. "You're drawing lines downhill. If you go over mountains, you should draw uphill."

"It's only a map," Ida said. "It doesn't matter how you draw lines on a map."

"Yes, it does," insisted Norman. "I'll bet Honey Bunch will get lost if she doesn't know any better than that. You have to draw lines uphill when you are going over mountains on a map."

But the little girls all declared that it didn't matter, and Honey Bunch said she wouldn't get lost with her daddy to take care of her, and finally Norman stopped talking about the map and instead asked questions about what they would see along the road and how long they would be gone and whether Honey Bunch would be afraid to sleep outdoors at night.

"I don't know how long we'll be gone," said Honey Bunch patiently. "I forgot to ask Daddy. And we'll see lots of things. I remember when we went to visit my cousin, Stub, we saw ever so many things, and people, too."

When Ida and the others had gone home it seemed to Honey Bunch that the best thing for her to do would be to ask some questions. All her friends were curious about her trip, and she had slipped away from the luncheon table so quickly that she had not learned much except that they were going on the Royal Green and Blue Tour.

Honey Bunch went into the house and

found Mother busily sorting clean clothes spread out on the bed in the guest room.

"Mother, when are we going?" asked Honey Bunch, peeping in at the door.

"Three days from to-day," Mrs. Morton answered, shaking something out of the pocket of a khaki blouse.

"That's my camping blouse, isn't it, Mother?" said Honey Bunch, remembering the days she had spent in camp. "What is in the pocket?"

"Pine needles," replied Mrs. Morton, smiling. "I thought the blouse would be just the thing for you to wear in the car, dear."

"But Eleanor hasn't a camping suit," said Honey Bunch anxiously. "Ida Grace has, only her clothes won't fit Eleanor. And I said the next doll to go on a trip should be Eleanor. I promised her."

"We'll find something for Eleanor to wear," Mrs. Morton promised. "Of course it will never do to disappoint her. Stub will like to see her, too."

"Stub?" echoed Honey Bunch. "Are we

going to see Stub? On the farm, Mother? Does she know it?"

Mrs. Morton laughed and began to look over a pile of tan socks that belonged to Honey Bunch.

"You sound like Norman Clark, Honey Bunch," she teased. "Yes, we are going to stop and see Stub. You'll like that, won't you?"

Honey Bunch dearly loved her cousin Stub, and she was delighted at the prospect of seeing her again. Stub lived on a farm and Honey Bunch had had a wonderful time there when she visited her.

"Oh, I forgot!" said Honey Bunch, remembering Norman's question. "How long shall we be gone, Mother?"

"Daddy said he thought about a month, dear," Mrs. Morton returned. "Are you getting ready to answer Norman's questions, Honey Bunch?"

Honey Bunch laughed. She liked Norman, but he was certainly famous among his friends for his ability to ask questions.

"But everybody says, 'When are you going and how long will you be away?'" declared Honey Bunch. "So I thought I ought to know, Mother."

"Yes, of course," her mother agreed, kissing her. "There is Mrs. Miller calling you, Honey Bunch."

"The clothes must be dry," said Honey Bunch, who was a very busy young person indeed from the time she woke up smiling in the morning until the time she went smiling to bed at night.

The clothes *were* dry. Mrs. Miller, as soon as she saw Honey Bunch, said that the exact moment had arrived for bringing in the wash.

"I don't believe in leaving clothes on the line, once they are sweet and dry," declared Mrs. Miller, picking up the basket with one hand and opening the screen door of the laundry with the other.

"No, I don't either," Honey Bunch said, trotting up the steps after her.

They had reached the top steps when there came the most awful clatter and banging against the fence and the whole fence swayed as though it were coming down in a heap.

"Ow!" shrieked Norman's voice. "Ow! Somebody come quick!"

"It's that young one!" said Mrs. Miller. "I never knew a boy who could make so much noise in my life!"

"He's hurt!" Honey Bunch cried in great distress, running to the fence. "Come get Norman, Mrs. Miller. He's hurt."

Mrs. Miller could not walk very swiftly and she could not run at all, she was so fat, but she hurried as much as she could. The fence was still swaying back and forth and Norman was evidently kicking against it with all his might.

"My land, he's caught!" said Mrs. Miller, standing on a flower-pot to see over.

CHAPTER VII

SOME PRESENTS

HONEY BUNCH danced around upon the ground, trying to peer through the cracks in the boards while Mrs. Miller stood on tiptoe on the flower-pot and looked over on the other side of the fence.

"Stop kicking," she commanded. "What's the matter with you?"

"My foot's caught!" Honey Bunch heard Norman answer. "It's fastened in that cleat— ow!"

Mrs. Miller had pushed his foot so suddenly that poor Norman, released, fell in a heap on top of his mother's nasturtium bed.

"Are you hurt, Norman?" called Honey Bunch. "Are you hurt a little bit?"

Mrs. Miller stepped down from the flowerpot and Norman scrambled up on top of the fence. His face was dirty and his hair was

more tumbled than usual, but he did not seem
to be hurt, and Honey Bunch was very glad
he was all right.

"Thank you for unhooking me, Mrs. Miller," said Norman politely. "My mother isn't
home and I might have had to stay there till
dinner time."

"Not if you made a noise like that," Mrs.
Miller replied, folding up a pillowcase and
putting it in her basket. "The fire depart-
ment would have been here in another minute."

"I was coming to see you, Honey Bunch,"
said Norman, "to tell you about Uncle Lysander."

"Uncle Lysander?" Honey Bunch repeated,
puzzled.

"Yes, you know—the uncle we saw in short
pants," said Norman. "Well, I told my
mother about him, and she had one when she
was a little girl. An uncle like that, I mean.
She had an Uncle Mortimer who was only
three years older than she was—he was her
mother's little brother."

"Well, I suppose he was an uncie," Honey Bunch admitted. "But I would rather have nice big uncles like my Uncle Peter."

"I was bringing you something, Honey Bunch," said Norman, feeling in his pocket. "Bet I dropped it out—no, here it is."

He slipped down from the fence and came over to Honey Bunch.

"See, it's a compass," he explained, holding out something round and shining on his hand.

"A compass?" Honey Bunch asked doubtfully, not offering to touch the round thing.

"You can't get lost with a compass," said Norman. "You put it in your pocket and wherever you are—wherever you are, you can go somewhere else."

Honey Bunch said, "Oh!"

"A compass tells you where the north is, Honey Bunch," Mrs. Miller, who was busily folding the clean clothes, near by, explained. "The little needle always points to the north, and that way you can get your bearings and find your way about."

Honey Bunch didn't see how she should

find her way about by knowing where the
north was, but she didn't wish to ask questions
about this mysterious compass.

"Is the compass for me, Norman?" she
asked instead.

"Yes, I meant to give it to you," Norman
assured her. "Put it in your pocket and use
it on the Royal Green and Blue Tour. But
you have to tip it—if you don't tip it, it won't
work."

Honey Bunch took the compass and tipped
it. The needle spun round and pointed north,
so Norman said.

"Thank you very much," Honey Bunch
murmured happily. "I'll keep it in the pocket
of my khaki blouse."

"You aren't going to take your new game
with you, are you, Honey Bunch?" asked Norman anxiously.

"My chicken game?" said Honey Bunch.
"No; I'm only going to take Eleanor and the
rabbit."

"Then wouldn't you like me to keep the
chicken game for you till you come back?"

HONEY BUNCH DREW HER MAP

Honey Bunch : Her First Auto Tour.   *Page 67*

suggested Norman. "Some of the pieces might get lost."

"I'll go get it for you now," Honey Bunch offered. "It's a nice game, Norman, and you'll like to play it."

"Well, I thought I could take care of it for you while you were away," said Norman, sitting down on the steps to wait.

Honey Bunch flew into the house and pulled the chicken game out of the window seat drawer where she kept her toys. It was a new game Uncle Peter had sent her, and there was a wheel to spin and different colored counters. Honey Bunch liked to look at it more than she liked to play it. Her mother said it was a little too old for her, and that may have been the reason she had not played it often. But Norman thought it was a fine game.

"Mother," called Honey Bunch, stopping on the stair landing with the game in her arms, "I just had a flash."

"You had a what?" Mrs. Morton asked, coming to the door of the guest room and looking a little puzzled.

"A flash," repeated Honey Bunch. "I'm going to name the rabbit 'Uncle Lysander.' Then he will remind me of the uncle in short pants."

Mrs. Morton thought that was a very good name for the velvet rabbit, and so did Norman and Mrs. Miller when they heard it. Norman took the game and went back over the fence and before dinner had played it three times with Teddy Gray.

Honey Bunch took the compass in to her mother and saw it put away in the pocket of her khaki blouse, all ready for the journey. Eleanor was to wear a blue dress and a pink sweater, and Mrs. Morton said that was a sensible outfit for her, because it was light and warm and could be washed.

There was a little more to be done each day, to get ready for the tour. Honey Bunch and Mother and Mrs. Miller had to do most of the work, for of course Daddy Morton was busy at his office. Honey Bunch sometimes wondered if he put covers on the chairs and pulled down the shades and dusted off the inkwells and hid the pens and pencils till he should come back. But when she asked Mother, Mrs. Morton said no indeed, that Daddy had to plan out work for the other people in his office to do and he had to write letters telling other folks that he would be away and he had to do as much work in advance as he could, so that business would run smoothly when he was not there.

"My, that's a lot to do," sighed Honey Bunch.

"It's a sight easier to take care of a house than an office, Honey Bunch," said Mrs. Miller, and Honey Bunch was sure of that.

She had told Lady Clare all about their trip, and the cat was quite willing to stay with Mrs. Miller. Honey Bunch thought that Lady Clare ought to be used to visiting Mrs. Miller by this time. Whenever the Mortons went away, Lady Clare was sent to stay with Mrs. Miller, and she always had a beautiful time. She had her own special rocking chair and cushion and a china saucer with blue roses on it, and if she had been on a trip to

London to see the queen—like the cat in the
nursery rhyme that Honey Bunch liked to say
to Lady Clare—she could not have had more
attention paid to her. She liked it, too. Lady
Clare liked to be petted.

The trunk that fitted on the back of the new
car was brought into the house and Honey
Bunch and her mother spent several busy
hours packing it. They didn't take many
"best" clothes, because when you are touring
you do not wear white dresses and pink sashes
—you know that. You wear sensible, strong
clothes that will not be ruined by sun or rain.
Yet Mrs. Morton said there would be times
when a pretty dress would be useful, so she
packed a few that belonged to Honey Bunch
and put in one or two for herself. Honey
Bunch put in Eleanor's best blue dress, too,
because she said that Stub's dolls might expect their guest to look extra nice. Not that
Stub played with dolls very much—she was an
outdoor girl and far more apt to go wading
in the brook than plan a tea party for her dolls
and their visitor.

Norman Clark and Ida Camp, because they
lived so near, tried to help, and while Mrs.
Miller declared that she could work faster
alone, both Mrs. Morton and Honey Bunch
thought it was lovely of the two chums to wish
to be helpful, and even when they made mis-
takes Mrs. Morton was patient.

"I'm awfully sorry, Honey Bunch," said
Norman, the afternoon before the time set for
Honey Bunch to start, "but I lost one of the
counters of your chicken game. And I think
I know where it is."

"Then that's all right," Honey Bunch, who
was struggling to put Eleanor's sweater on
(the doll's head was larger than the opening,
and you know what trouble *that* makes).
"The counter isn't really lost, if you know
where it is."

"Well, I can't get it," said Norman. "It
rolled down the sewer at the corner. I was
coming home from Lester's and I had the
counters in my pocket—one dropped out while
I was just holding them in my hand to look at."

"Never mind," Honey Bunch comforted

him. "You can take care of the others, can't you, Norman?"

Norman said he could and he sat on the fence and drummed with his heels against the boards till Mrs. Miller came out and asked him if he didn't have anything to do.

"I'm waiting for Ida," said Norman. "She is going to bring Honey Bunch a present. She said she was coming right over."

A present sounded exciting, and Honey Bunch finished pulling on Eleanor's sweater a little more hastily than she would have done if she had not been wondering what Ida was bringing her.

"Lady Clare ought to have a present," said Mrs. Miller good-naturedly. "The cover of her basket is loose, and I've had to tie it on with string. I don't believe it will last longer than this one trip."

Lady Clare was always put in a basket with a cover on it to go to Mrs. Miller's house. The cat didn't like the basket, but it was the only way the washerwoman could safely carry her through the streets.

"Here comes Ida!" called Norman, jumping down from the fence.

Ida came through the side yard and in her hands she was carefully carrying a package wrapped in white paper. You would have known it was a present the moment you saw it. It was even tied with pink string.

Honey Bunch tried not to stare at the package, but Norman kept nudging her to take it. He was anxious to see what it was.

"I brought you something to use on your tour, Honey Bunch," said Ida, handing the package to her chum. "They're handkerchiefs to tell you the days."

"Oh, my!" Honey Bunch murmured, untying the pink string.

She found a white box, and when she lifted the lid, there were seven handkerchiefs, one on top of the other. Each was a different color and each had a different picture in the corner.

"If you forget what day it is while you are touring," Ida explained, "you look at your handkerchief and you can tell right away.

There is a little girl washing for Monday and ironing for Tuesday and something for every day in the week."

"They're lovely," said Honey Bunch, giving Ida a kiss. "Now I have some handkerchiefs and a compass."

So Ida looked at the compass and Norman took out all the handkerchiefs and looked at them. He said he liked the Friday handkerchief best because it was pink.

"I like blue and so does Honey Bunch," declared Ida.

"I hear the telephone!" cried Mrs. Miller, as a shrill ringing sounded from inside the house. "You go, Honey Bunch—your mother is at the top of the house."

CHAPTER VIII

SOMETHING SAD HAPPENS

HONEY BUNCH could answer the telephone nicely and she liked to do it. She ran into the house now and Norman stood with his nose pressed against the screen door so that he could see her, if she left the door open, and listen. Norman liked to listen to any one telephone.

But Honey Bunch did not pay any attention to the kitchen door, and it closed behind her. Though Norman listened carefully, he could not hear a word.

"Who was it? What did they want? Was it some one for your mother?" asked Norman, as soon as Honey Bunch came out on the back steps again.

"It was Daddy," Honey Bunch reported. "Mrs. Miller, Daddy says to take Lady Clare to your house this afternoon. He's coming up right away."

Mrs. Morton, who had come downstairs and talked to Honey Bunch's daddy, too, opened the screen door.

"Mr. Morton wants to make an earlier start in the morning than we planned at first, Mrs. Miller," she said. "He is going to bring the car up, and he'd like to take everything over to your house that is to go there. He says he can take the clothes basket just as it is, and when we send you the address you can forward us the clean things."

Norman didn't understand about the clothes basket, but Honey Bunch did. Sometimes when they were going away, Mrs. Miller took the clean clothes that she did not have time to iron home with her and ironed them there and later sent them neatly packed in a box to Mrs. Morton.

"Well," said Mrs. Miller comfortably, "it's lucky I didn't dampen the clothes. I'll leave the basket right out here in the yard. Where's Lady Clare?"

No one knew. Honey Bunch was sure she

had seen her cat sitting on the fence a little while before and Norman said he had seen her crawl under the steps, but though they called, "Lady Clare! Lady Clare!" and "Kitty, kitty, here, kitty!" no black cat with a collar of ermine fur around her pretty neck came out to greet them.

"I told her about going, but of course I said we were going to-morrow morning," said Honey Bunch. "Lady Clare may have gone to see some of her friends. She didn't know Daddy would want her to be ready so soon."

Daddy Morton drove up in the car just then, and he called for Lady Clare, too, but still the cat didn't come.

"I'll take Mrs. Miller's clothes-basket and any packages," he decided at last, "and while I am gone, you hunt for the cat. If possible, I want Mrs. Miller to take her to-night. We are going early in the morning, and I will not have any time to make another trip."

There were several packages and two or

three plants, besides the clothes-basket, to go
in the car. Mrs. Miller always took care of
Honey Bunch's mother's pretty house plants
when the house was shut up.

"See if you children can't find Lady Clare,"
said Mr. Morton, as he drove away.

"I can find her," boasted Norman. "I'm
going to climb all the fences on this block, and
I'll bet I find her somewhere."

"You be nice to her," Honey Bunch told
him quickly. "Lady Clare doesn't like to be
scolded."

Norman said he wouldn't scold and he
started off to climb the fences. He stepped on
a great many flower beds, and some of the people into whose yards he climbed were not at
all pleased to see him. But Norman kept
right on, scrambling up and down, calling
"kitty, kitty," as he hunted.

Honey Bunch thought for a few moments
before she determined what to do. She tried
to think where Lady Clare would go, and at
last she decided that she might have gone
around the corner to sit on the grating.

"The grating?" repeated Mrs. Miller, when
Honey Bunch told her that. "What grating?"

Mrs. Miller had stayed to help hunt for the
cat, and she was going around the house, the
basket in her hand, in case she should find
Lady Clare suddenly, and then she could pop
her into the basket. Mrs. Miller was so stout
that it was hard for her to bend down and
look, but she tried to see under the steps and
she looked behind boxes in the cellar, though
it made her face very red to stoop so much.

"There is a grating, you know, around the
corner," Honey Bunch explained. "It is
under the bakery window. Lady Clare lies
down on it sometimes."

"To be sure," returned Mrs. Miller.
"That is where the ovens are; and even in the
dead of summer a cat can not get too much
heat. Well, maybe Lady Clare is around
there—you'll go see, won't you, Honey
Bunch?"

Honey Bunch said of course she would, and
she trotted around to the bakery. It wasn't

far, and as long as she did not have to cross
any streets, she was allowed to go without first
asking Mother.

"I knew it," said Honey Bunch to herself
as soon as she reached the corner. "I knew
Lady Clare would be there."

Lady Clare was comfortably curled up on
the warm grating, her front paws neatly
tucked under her and her pink nose just rest-
ing on the iron bars.

"Lady Clare, Daddy wants you to go to
Mrs. Miller's right away," said Honey Bunch
firmly.

Lady Clare opened her eyes and blinked.
Perhaps she had been having a beautiful kitty
dream in which she had dozens of mice to
play with and saucers of cream for her dinner. Anyway, she looked very pleasant and
very sleepy.

Honey Bunch picked her up and tucked her
under her arm and they started back to the
house.

"I found her!" called Honey Bunch, as she
came in sight of her yard and saw Mrs. Mil-

ler on her knees, trying to peer under the lawn
mower.

Not that Lady Clare would be likely to hide
under the lawn mower, but, as Mrs. Miller
explained, she had looked everywhere else.

"My land, Honey Bunch, I certainly am
glad to see that cat," said Mrs. Miller. "Let's
put her in the basket this minute and then
we'll be ready when your daddy comes back."

Lady Clare didn't like her basket much. It
ruffled her fur and her feelings to be hidden
away inside it, with the lid tied down. But
the only time Mrs. Miller had tried to carry
her to her house without the basket, Lady
Clare had been so frightened at the automobiles and trolley cars and crowds of people
that she had scratched and spit and generally
behaved so badly that Mrs. Miller said she
would never, *never,* NEVER try to take her
again unless she was in a basket.

Mrs. Morton came out to see Lady Clare,
and she held her and stroked her gently while
Mrs. Miller brought the basket and Honey
Bunch held up the cover.

"Never mind, Lady Clare, you won't have to stay in the basket very long," whispered Mrs. Morton, putting the cat into the basket very carefully and patting her so that she would not be frightened.

"You'll be all right as soon as you see your rocking chair and the nice supper I'll have ready for you," Mrs. Miller promised.

"You like to stay with Mrs. Miller, Lady Clare, you know you do," said Honey Bunch, putting down the cover of the basket.

Before she could fasten it the side gate creaked and in came Norman, dragging something on a string. As soon as he was through the gate a small yellow dog shot ahead of him and began to drag Norman.

"Woof!" barked the dog loudly. "Woof! Woof!"

"He's a bloodhound!" Norman shouted. "I borrowed him from another boy."

"Spitz whiz me-ow-w!" said Lady Clare furiously.

The basket rocked, fell down the steps, the lid flew open, and out flew Lady Clare, her

"I FOUND HER!" CALLED HONEY BUNCH.

Honey Bunch : Her First Auto Tour.   *Page* 90

eyes glaring and her soft fur standing on end. Honey Bunch stared at her tail in astonishment. Why, Lady Clare's tail was as large as a rolling pin!

"Stop her!" gasped Mrs. Miller. "Norman Clark, take that dog away! Somebody catch the cat, quick!"

But Lady Clare had reached the fence, climbed it, and disappeared.

"What do you mean, bringing a dog in here where you know a cat is—or was?" scolded Mrs. Miller.

Norman looked surprised.

"How did I know you'd found her?" he asked. "I was hunting all over for Lady Clare, and down the street I met Paul Downing and he said he had a bloodhound that could find anything. So I thought perhaps I could use the dog to find Lady Clare."

The "bloodhound" was pulling at the string and whining. He wanted to climb the fence, too, and chase Lady Clare. But Norman held him fast and would not let him go.

Suddenly Mrs. Morton sat down on the

steps and began to laugh. She laughed so
hard the tears came into her eyes and she was
still laughing when Mr. Morton drove up in
the car. She was laughing so much she
couldn't tell him what had happened, but
Honey Bunch did.

"Lady Clare was around under the bakery
window, Daddy," said Honey Bunch. "I
found her and brought her home and we had
her all packed, but Norman brought a bloodhound into the yard and she was frightened
and ran away."

"A—a bloodhound, did you say?" asked
Mr. Morton, staring at the yellow dog.

"Yes, sir. I thought perhaps he'd help us
find the cat," Norman explained.

And then Mr. Morton began to laugh, too,
and Honey Bunch and Norman wondered
what could be so funny.

Mrs. Miller didn't laugh, though.

"No telling where that cat has gone now,"
she grumbled, "or when we will ever get it
back."

Honey Bunch looked anxious.

"Oh, we have to find her!" she exclaimed. "We can't go away and leave Lady Clare outdoors."

"We'll find her," said Mrs. Morton quickly. "Mrs. Miller and I will go ahead and finish packing, Honey Bunch, but you and Norman stay outdoors and look for Lady Clare. Only keep the dog out of sight, Norman. Lady Clare won't come home if she thinks a strange dog is in her yard."

Though Honey Bunch searched and called till dinner time and went to the bakery grating three separate times, she could not find Lady Clare. Her daddy was sure the cat would come home that night.

"I'll leave Uncle Lysander out in the grass for her, and perhaps she will come and chew his ears," said Honey Bunch hopefully.

CHAPTER IX

TIME TO START

EVERY one was up extra early in the house the next morning, to get ready for the trip, but Honey Bunch was the first one downstairs, and she ran out into the side yard to see if Lady Clare had come back.

Uncle Lysander, the velvet rabbit, lay in the grass just as she had placed him, but his ears were quite as smooth as they had ever been. No Lady Clare had been nibbling them, that was plain.

"Lady Clare didn't come home!" said Honey Bunch, going slowly into the kitchen where her mother was getting breakfast.

Tears gathered in the little girl's blue eyes.

"She's lost," sobbed Honey Bunch. "My kitty is lost and I love her very much and she loves me."

"Why, darling, don't cry like that," Mrs.

96

Morton said, putting her arm around her little girl. "I'll tell you what we will do—
Mrs. Miller will come every day to the house
to see if Lady Clare is here. Just as soon as
she stops being frightened, I am sure she will
come back. And we'll leave a saucer and
plate for her on the back porch and Mrs. Miller shall keep them filled with food and water,
so when Lady Clare comes she will know that
we are expecting her and she won't go away
again."

Mrs. Miller came just then to help the Mortons, as she always did when they were going
away, and she promised faithfully to come
every day and see if Lady Clare had come
back.

"Every single day, Honey Bunch," promised Mrs. Miller. "Rain or shine, I'll walk
around and watch for Lady Clare. And I
will see that there is always food in her dish
and water in her saucer for her, so don't you
fret a mite. We'll find her for you."

Honey Bunch felt better right away and
she put a saucer of water out on the back

porch and a plate with oatmeal and milk on
it, all ready for Lady Clare, before she ate her
own breakfast.

If it hadn't been for the lost cat, Honey
Bunch would have found the next two hours
most exciting. She trotted around after her
daddy while he locked doors and windows
and pulled down the shades and carried things
out to the car. Honey Bunch carried out
Eleanor, in her sweater, and she took Uncle
Lysander and put him on the back seat, to
keep Eleanor company.

"Have you got the handkerchiefs?" asked
Ida Camp, when she came to say good-bye.

"Don't forget the compass," Norman Clark
told her, when he climbed over the fence to
say good-bye.

Honey Bunch had a handkerchief in one
hand and the compass in the other, as she
showed them, and if she put them down a moment to help her daddy, she picked them up
again as soon as she had finished.

Presently the house was all ready to leave,
every door locked but the front one, every

window-shade down, all the furniture neatly covered so that it would not get dusty. Honey Bunch and her mother went out to the car and got in and Mr. Morton locked the front door while Mrs. Miller stood on the curb and talked.

"I'll be back in a minute," Honey Bunch murmured.

She slipped down from the seat and ran through the yard, while Norman and Ida stared after her. Honey Bunch took a hasty look at the plate and saucer—nothing had been touched.

"Lady Clare hasn't come back," she told her daddy, who was waiting for her at the gate.

"Never mind, Mrs. Miller will find her," he said, and he seemed so sure of it that Honey Bunch also felt sure.

"Here come the others," said Ida, and down the street, pell-mell, rushed a group of girls and boys, eager to see Honey Bunch "start touring," as Kitty Williams said.

They lined up on the curb—Kitty and Cora Williams and Fannie Graham and Mary, her

sister, and Lester Fox and Paul Niles, and they
waved their hands and cried, "Good-bye,
Honey Bunch—good-bye, Honey Bunch," as
the car started.

They were half way down the block when
Norman shouted something after them.

Mr. Morton stopped the car and glanced
back.

"What did he say?" he asked, frowning a
little.

Honey Bunch put her head out of the car
and called to Norman.

"What did you say?" she called. "Norman,
what did you say?"

Norman made a tube of his hands and
shouted again.

"I—lost—another—one of your—counters!" he screamed. "You know! One of the
counters—from—your chicken game!"

"Norman lost another counter from my
chicken game," said Honey Bunch.

"Tell him all right, that's very nice, and
then we can go on," her daddy said.

This made Mrs. Morton laugh, but Honey

Bunch leaned out again and called to Norman. "All right, Norman—that's nice," and before she could tell whether he had heard her or not the car went on and in a few minutes they were so far away that no matter how loudly Norman shouted, they would not have heard him.

"Now we are really going, aren't we?" said Honey Bunch, with satisfaction.

"We are really going," her daddy agreed. "And I wonder if any one can tell me where we're going."

"I know! Broad Acres!" cried Honey Bunch eagerly. "And we are going to see Stub and Liny and Michael and Aunt Carol and Uncle Rand—and everybody."

Honey Bunch, you see, had visited at the farm before and she remembered the good times she had had there with Stub, who was her cousin.

"Are we going over the same road, Daddy?" she asked, "The very same road?"

"Unless we have to make a detour, we'll go the same way, I think," her daddy answered.

"Maybe we'll see Ruth Evans, then," said Honey Bunch.

Neither her mother nor her daddy remembered Ruth Evans till Honey Bunch reminded them that she was the little girl who had come down to the letter box to see if the postman had left her any letters.

"Perhaps you'll see her, and if you don't, we'll drop a note in the mail box," said Mrs. Morton smiling. "You'd like to surprise Ruth, wouldn't you, Honey Bunch?"

Of course Honey Bunch loved to surprise people, and she thought it would be great fun to leave a note for Ruth, if they did not see her. Honey Bunch remembered the people they had met on their way to Stub's home, and her daddy remembered the road, and they reached the Morgan hotel where they were to have dinner without having to look at the road maps once.

Honey Bunch was a bit disappointed that every one in the dining room was "different" —by that she meant she saw no one she had seen on her first visit there. But she forgot her disappointment when her mother asked her what to say in the note to Ruth.

"I'll write it now and then we shall not have to ask Daddy to wait when we come to the mail box," Mrs. Morton explained.

So Honey Bunch told her mother to give her love to Ruth and to tell her they were going to see Stub again and to ask her if her Cousin Laura was coming to see her soon.

"You remember everything, don't you, Honey Bunch?" said her mother, smiling as she wrote the note.

They finished their lunch and went back to the car and Honey Bunch began to look for the mail box right away. She remembered that Ruth did not live very far from the hotel, though she did live in the country where there were no houses to be seen.

"I see it!" cried Honey Bunch, almost falling out of the car as she pointed to the white box nailed to a post. "Look, Daddy, that is Ruth Evans' mail box. But I don't see Ruth," she added sadly.

"She may have gone to visit her cousin

Laura," Daddy Morton suggested. "Put in
the letter, Honey Bunch, and bend up the
flag, and then some one will surely see it and
send it to Ruth if she isn't at home."

Honey Bunch leaned out of the car and
opened the mail box. She put in the note her
mother had written and bent the tiny red flag
so that it stood upright. This, she knew, meant
that there was something in the box, and who-
ever came to get the mail would know there
was a letter there.

"Now," said Honey Bunch, as her daddy
swung the car into the wide oiled road again,
"let's go see Mr. and Mrs. Popover."

Mrs. Morton looked at her husband and
laughed.

"Honey Bunch, I believe you could find
your way to Stub's house alone," said her
daddy. "I had forgotten all about the Popovers."

"I was speaking to Mrs. Miller about them
a few weeks ago," Honey Bunch's mother said,
"and I called them Mr. and Mrs. Bunn."

Honey Bunch remembered Mr. and Mrs.

Popover very well. She and her mother and daddy had stopped at their house during a thunderstorm and there had been a basket of kittens to play with and cookies to eat.

"They said to come again," urged Honey Bunch, trying not to think about the kittens, because they made her think of Lady Clare.

And they would probably have gone to see Mr. and Mrs. Popover and Honey Bunch would have had a chance to see the kittens, now grown up to be big cats, if a large sign had not caught her daddy's eyes.

"Detour!" he cried. "We might have known. That will mean six or seven extra miles."

"We can't stop and see the Popovers this time, dear," explained Honey Bunch's mother. "The road which leads past their house is closed for repairs. We have to go around a different way. Perhaps on the way back we can stop."

Honey Bunch was disappointed, but she did not grumble. Not for nothing was she called "Honey Bunch."

"I'll take Uncle Lysander up here so he can see a little better," she decided. "After he has had a little change, I'll hold Eleanor."

She managed to reach over and catch Uncle Lysander by one of his long velvet ears. He sat up nicely in her lap and seemed to enjoy the scenery. Once Daddy Morton declared he was wrinkling his nose.

"A-ha! I see what the trouble is," said Honey Bunch's daddy. "That is a field of carrots we are passing. Any rabbit will wrinkle his nose when he sees carrots. If we had more time we'd stop and get Uncle Lysander one."

But they didn't stop, for they were anxious to reach Broad Acres in time for the five o'clock supper. The cars they passed seemed to be going slowly, and in several of them the passengers were studying road maps.

"Here's another detour," said Mrs. Morton suddenly. "Oh, David, that looks like a narrow lane. I don't believe we have to go that way. It's a dirt road, too!"

But Honey Bunch's daddy said there was

no other way to go, and he turned in carefully at the weed-choked road that did look like a lane.

He was driving slowly when the car gave a sudden lurch. Honey Bunch clutched her mother and Uncle Lysander sailed over the wind shield and disappeared. The car gave another lurch and seemed to be tipping to one side.

"Ditched!" said Mr. Morton, as the car stopped with a jolt.

CHAPTER X

HONEY BUNCH AND STUB

"UNCLE LYSANDER fell out!" quavered Honey Bunch, a little frightened.

"We'll find him," her daddy answered cheerfully. "I think you girls had better get out; no telling how far in we are. I'll have to get help."

He opened the door on the side of the car nearest the road and lifted down Honey Bunch, then her mother. They could see now that two of the wheels were deep in a ditch at the side of the road.

"The first thing to do is to find Uncle Lysander," said Mr. Morton seriously. "Then I'll have to hunt up a team of good old-fashioned horses."

"Uncle Rand has horses," Honey Bunch said hopefully. "If we were only there, he would lend them to us."

"But we are miles away from the farm, dear," her mother reminded her.

"I don't see what makes this road so soft," she added, speaking to Mr. Morton.

The road was sticky and soft and the land on either side of it was not like any land Honey Bunch had ever seen. It was not woods or green fields, but brown, bare stretches of earth with here and there little pools of water and perhaps a few patches of grass.

They heard the rattle of wheels now, and coming toward them was an old, worn buggy without a top and pulled by a black mule. An old man was driving. He stopped a few feet away from them, picked up something, climbed back into the buggy and jogged on toward them.

"He's found Uncle Lysander," whispered Honey Bunch.

"Did you lose a bean bag?" the old man called, stopping his mule a few feet from Honey Bunch, who pressed back against her mother.

The mule had ears as long as Uncle Lysander's, but he did not look nearly so pleasant. In fact he looked as though he might be cross.

"That's Uncle Lysander," Mr. Morton explained gravely. "Thank you very much, sir. Can you tell me where I can get a team to haul us out of here?"

"I'll come back soon as I get my stock fed," said the old man. "My team of mules can haul out anything."

"Well—of course we'll have to wait," Mr. Morton said. "There doesn't seem to be any farms around here. What section is this? We had to detour, and I am not familiar with the road."

"They're filling it in—used to be swamp land," replied the old man, slapping the lines on his mule to start him. "Just got this road through last month. Most folks go round the other way—guess the detour sign got turned around. The boys do that once in a while for a joke."

He jogged on and Honey Bunch and her mother and daddy sat down on the running

board of the car to wait. Mrs. Miller had
packed a lunch for them, and they ate it for
their supper. The old man did not come back
and no other car passed them.

"We'll not get to Stub's in time for supper,
shall we?" said Honey Bunch, as she munched
a sandwich thoughtfully.

"We'll not get there for breakfast, unless
that man hurries a bit," her daddy declared
impatiently. "I'm going to see if I can't get
out of here myself."

Honey Bunch and her mother stood at one
side of the road and waited while he started
the engine. But the wheels, deep in the mud
and water of the ditch, refused to respond.

"No use—we'll have to wait," said Mr.
Morton. "I'd go and try to find a farm, but
I don't like the idea of leaving you two alone
on this road."

"Let's wait," Mrs. Morton begged, and they
waited till it was dark and the moon came up
and queer little insects chirped in the weeds
that grew along the roadside.

"That man has probably forgotten all about

us," said Mrs. Morton. "We'll have to camp out. Honey Bunch is going to sleep in my lap."

The car lamps were lit, and it did not take Honey Bunch's daddy long to put up the tent and unfold the cots. True, they had not meant to camp in the middle of the road, but the middle of the road, if there is no traffic, is just as comfortable as a meadow. Honey Bunch had Eleanor and Uncle Lysander for company in her cot and she went to sleep at once and only woke up once in the night when the moon shone in through the door of the tent. But it was such a jolly smiling moon she didn't mind that and was soon asleep again.

They were all up early the next morning, and, more than anything else, they wanted a drink of water. There was nothing to cook on the stove, so Mrs. Morton could not get breakfast, but she had saved an apple for Honey Bunch, who ate it hungrily.

It was a sunny day. Indeed, by the time the **tent** was rolled and everything put away neatly, the sun was too warm for comfort. Mr. Morton had made up his mind to walk to the nearest farm—no matter how far away it might be—when Honey Bunch pointed down the road.

"There comes a man," she cried.

It was the old man and his two mules, and when he came up to them he handed Mrs. Morton a covered tin pail.

"Thought you'd want a drink of water," he explained. "I couldn't come back last night, because my wife was afraid the night air would give me rheumatism."

He was so anxious to help them and he seemed to know just what to do and they were so glad to have the car pulled out of the ditch that no one said a word about the way he had left them the night before. As soon as he had the car on the road again, he asked them to come to his house for breakfast.

"My wife said to tell you to be sure and come," he urged. "We have hot cakes and maple sugar. The little girl will like maple sugar."

But Honey Bunch's daddy thanked him and said they must hurry on.

"We'll get breakfast somewhere along the way," said Mr. Morton, but Honey Bunch's mother was so afraid that Stub's mother would be worrying about them that she didn't want to stop even for breakfast.

So they drove ahead steadily, and in a few hours were turning in at the long shady drive that brought them to the farmhouse.

Stub was the first to see them, and she came racing over the lawn with a shout. She tripped once and fell—that was Stub; her nickname was given her because she was always falling down—but she scrambled up and hopped on one foot the rest of the way.

"Honey Bunch!" screamed Stub. "Oh, Mother, Honey Bunch has come and everybody!"

Almost before the car stopped, Stub was on the running board, and, glad as she was to see her cousin, she noticed the camping outfit, too.

"This isn't the car you had last time," she said quickly.

"The automobile man gave me a new car for the old one," explained Honey Bunch's daddy, who loved to tease his tomboy niece.

"I like this one better," said Stub.

By this time Stub's daddy and mother had come out and Honey Bunch was passed around like a little bag of sugar.

"Have you had breakfast?" asked Aunt Carol, who was Stub's pretty mother. "You haven't? Come right in! We sat up till midnight, hoping you would make it last night. Here's Buffy, Honey Bunch."

The big collie dog shook his paw gravely at Honey Bunch and she hugged him. Breakfast smelled delicious and tasted still better, though Stub could hardly wait for Honey Bunch to eat hers.

"We have to play," said Stub excitedly. "Michael wants to see you, too. And—oh, here's Liny!"

Liny was just as Honey Bunch remembered her—short and fat and with a beaming smile, and she was so glad to see Honey Bunch that she kissed her and dropped a biscuit into

her lap instead of on her plate. But Honey
Bunch didn't mind that—she was glad to see
Liny.

"Now we can play," said Stub, when Honey
Bunch had finished her breakfast.

Of course they headed straight for the barn.
That is the point of interest on any farm, and
Honey Bunch loved Uncle Rand's big cool
barn with the enormous haymow.

"'Lo, Honey Bunch!" a cheerful voice
called to her as she and Stub crossed the
chicken yard.

"Why, Michael—you nice Michael, how
glad I am to see you!" Honey Bunch cried in
delight.

Michael came and tossed her up almost to
the top of the dwarf cherry tree and said he
was just as glad to see her.

"As for Stub, she's been talking about you
for two weeks," said Michael. "She wants
you to spend the summer."

Stub and Honey Bunch visited all the farm
animals and slid down the hay several times
and Stub had just discovered Uncle Lysander

in the car when Liny came out to tell them
that dinner was ready.

"My goodness, we never can do anything
because we always have to stop to eat," com-
plained Stub. "Let's go berrying this afternoon, Honey Bunch, or you'll have to go home
before we have any fun."

"You and Honey Bunch must get all the
fun you can out of to-day, dear," said Aunt
Carol. "We can't get Uncle David and Aunt
Edith to stay any longer than that."

So then Stub said that Uncle Lysander must
go berrying with them, and he did. She carried him and Honey Bunch carried the two
tin pails, and they went down the road where
the sweetest blackberries Honey Bunch had
ever tasted grew. She remembered when she
had gone after berries at the camp, and as they
picked she told Stub about that time and of
how Ida Grace had been lost and was found.

"And now Lady Clare is lost," said Honey
Bunch sadly.

But when Stub heard about that, she said
she knew of a cat that had been lost for six

months and had come home Christmas morning.

"Cats hardly ever stay lost, Honey Bunch," said Stub, and of course Honey Bunch could not help feeling more cheerful after that.

The only thing that happened to them that afternoon was a slight accident to Stub. She dropped Uncle Lysander, and when she reached for him her elbow knocked over her pail of berries and she lost her own balance and fell into the berry bushes, which are, as you all know, very, very briary. Stub was a country girl and didn't mind a few scratches, and she escaped with less than some folks would, because she knew enough not to scramble around. She rose up with great care, pulled Uncle Lysander out with her, and declared that she wasn't going to bother to pick any more berries.

"Let's go home and slide on the hay," she suggested.

Honey Bunch stared a little. Stub was always wanting to do something else, but now it seemed as if she couldn't change her mind fast enough. Her eyes sparkled, her cheeks were crimson, and she seemed as though she were excited, though Honey Bunch could see nothing to be excited over.

Honey Bunch, rather warm and tired, followed Stub back to the farm, and they went up in the haymow to slide on the hay.

"This mow hasn't been touched—we'll slide over here," said Stub, choosing a corner of the loft where the hay was piled highest.

They took turns, and Honey Bunch was going down for the fourth time when she felt a sudden weight pressing on her shoulders.

"Look out!" shouted Stub. "Roll over—roll over, Honey Bunch—roll!"

Honey Bunch tried to roll, but something heavy and dark and choking with dust covered her completely. She gasped and began to wave her arms and legs wildly.

"Daddy!" Honey Bunch screamed.

CHAPTER XI

THE GYPSIES

HONEY BUNCH was sure she had stopped breathing. How could any one breathe, smothered under a mass of hay that shut out the light and air? As for Stub, she began to burrow in the hay and to call for Michael.

"Here, here, what's all this?" cried Michael, running into the barn and climbing the hay-mow ladder in three leaps. "Where's Honey Bunch?"

Well, Honey Bunch was under the hay, but he had her out in a minute, coughing and sputtering.

"You ought to know better than to play under the shelving, Stub," scolded Michael, as he began gently to dust Honey Bunch off. "You might have guessed the load would slide. You've knocked down about a ton of hay on one little girl. Poor Honey Bunch!"

But as soon as she was downstairs and Stub
had picked the long straws out of her hair and
she had had a drink of water, Honey Bunch
was all right again.

"You'd better go up to the house and play,"
advised Michael. "I thought you were going
after berries?"

"We did," Stub said impatiently. "We
can't do one thing all the time."

However, she went around to the front
porch and Honey Bunch followed her, wondering what made Stub act so queerly.

"There's nothing to do, Mother," com-
plained Stub, as soon as she saw her mother
and her Aunt Edith on the porch. "There's
nothing to do, unless I can tell Honey Bunch."

"After that I think you might as well."
Stub's mother smiled. "We can't have Honey
Bunch wondering what you are talking about."

Stub turned and threw her arms around
Honey Bunch.

"I'm going with you in the morning!" she
cried triumphantly. "I'm going with you in
the camping-out car. Mother said I could

go as far as my Great-Aunt Molly's. Won't
it be fun, Honey Bunch?"

"Love-ly!" Honey Bunch said, her pink
cheeks getting pinker with delight. "We can
sit on the back seat and you can hold Uncle
Lysander."

Stub, you see, didn't care much for dolls
and she wasn't very fond of Eleanor, but she
thought Uncle Lysander was beautiful.

It was Stub who was up first the next morning, and Michael's shout of laughter drew
every one to the front bedroom windows. He
had gone out with the milk pails to do his
milking and discovered Stub, fully dressed for
her journey, sitting in the car holding Uncle
Lysander, but sound asleep.

She woke up, of course, and came into the
house for breakfast, but she and Honey Bunch
were so eager to be traveling that if it had
not been for the two mothers and Liny, they
would have paid no attention to their good
cereal and cream.

"Where does Great-Aunt Molly live?"

asked Honey Bunch, when breakfast was over
at last and they were waiting for the grownups to say they might get into the car.

"It's before you get to Three Lakes," said
Stub. "But I can camp out one night with
you—Uncle David said so. And Mother and
Daddy are coming to get me at Great-Aunt
Molly's when I have to come home."

Daddy Morton was taking good things to
eat from the farm—eggs and bacon and home-
made bread and some vegetables. Michael
helped him put the food in the white refrig-
erator and there was a large piece of ice in it
also, from the icehouse. Stub wanted to help,
but, as she herself admitted, she usually
fell down when she was carrying eggs, so it
seemed safer to sit and hold Uncle Lysander
and talk to Honey Bunch.

"All aboard for the Royal Green and Blue
Tour!" called Daddy Morton presently. "All
a-board! Are you ladies going on the tour?"
he asked Honey Bunch and Stub gravely,
while Mrs. Morton took her place and Uncle

Rand and Aunt Carol and Michael and Liny stood on the concrete carriage block and watched.

Honey Bunch giggled.

"Of course we're going," she said. "And Eleanor and Uncle Lysander are going, too."

"Well, hop in and I'll see your tickets later," said Daddy Morton, lifting Honey Bunch in without opening the door and swinging Stub in beside her.

There was a great flurry of kissing and handshaking and warnings from pretty Aunt Carol to Stub that she must be a good girl and not tear her frocks and to let Honey Bunch do some of the talking—it was Michael said that—and then the car swept down the driveway and out into the main road.

Honey Bunch and Stub smiled at each other. This was fun!

They laughed and chattered and told each other stories until Mrs. Morton glanced at her wrist watch and said it was noon. Stub was a little disappointed that the stove wasn't used or the tent put up, but her uncle explained that she should see all that when they stopped for supper.

"Just now I want to make a certain point and I can't afford to take too much time," said Mr. Morton. "We'll have our lunch picnic fashion and you girls may be gypsies this evening, if you wish."

Lunch was soon over and Honey Bunch and Stub went to sleep on the back seat and didn't know when the car stopped. They woke up to see Honey Bunch's daddy and mother studying a large road map spread across their knees.

"We're on the wrong road—that much is sure," Daddy Morton was saying, as Honey Bunch opened her blue eyes. "The question is, shall we go forward or turn around and try to puzzle out that fork back at the last sign post?"

"Are we lost, Daddy?" asked Honey Bunch excitedly, letting Eleanor slip to the floor as she struggled to sit up. "Daddy, are we lost? Because if we are, I have the compass Norman gave me, you know."

Stub was wide awake in a minute and demanded to see the compass. Honey Bunch had it in the pocket of her blouse, but though she tipped it as Norman had told her to do, and the needle swung around and showed, so Honey Bunch said, where the north was, Daddy Morton decided that he would rather trust to his road map.

"I wouldn't turn back," said Mrs. Morton. "We are going to camp out to-night anyway, and this road is bordered by deep meadows. Why not find a place and stop? Then in the morning you'll be rested and can make up any time you have lost."

They were passing a long green lane just then and a comfortable white farmhouse, something like the one Stub lived in, was not far off. Mr. Morton drove into the lane and left the car standing while he went to ask if the farmer were willing for campers to spend a night on his land.

"Perfectly satisfactory," he reported, coming back in a few minutes, smiling. "We're to take down the bars and go into the meadow.

Mr. Philbrick says he is glad to see us because there is a tribe of gypsies down the road a bit and he has been feeling sorry ever since he refused them permission to camp here."

He took down the bars and put them up again after he had driven the car through. There was a brook in the meadow and some weeping willow trees beside it which made a beautiful place for a camp. Honey Bunch was reminded of the children who had come to see them the first time they put up the tent, and especially of the uncle in short pants. She told Stub all about him. But Stub was more interested in the tent and the stove, and she almost fell into the corn kettle, so eager was she to see how corn looked when it was cooking out of doors.

Honey Bunch and Stub went up to the farmhouse, hand-in-hand, to get fresh milk for their supper—since they couldn't have any of the coffee that did smell so good bubbling in the tin coffee pot—and when they came back, they had a great deal to say about gypsies.

"Daddy, they're down the road," Honey Bunch reported. "They live outdoors all the time, even in winter. I never saw a gypsy. Did you?"

"Come and eat your supper, and if you are not too tired, perhaps we shall walk down past their camp before you have to go to bed," said Mrs. Morton, who had the little table set as neatly as though it had been in the dining room at home. There was even a bunch of wild flowers in the center of it.

Honey Bunch and Stub dried the dishes neatly after supper and then, as no one was the least bit sleepy, they all walked down the road to find the gypsy camp. Honey Bunch and Stub kept rather close to Mr. Morton, because they were not sure what gypsies did. Stub whispered that perhaps they jumped at you.

"There they are," said Mrs. Morton, when a turn in the road brought them in sight of a group of horses and wagons.

Honey Bunch stared. So did Stub. The gypsies had built a large fire and they were

grouped around it. Their horses were graz-
ing near them, and the wagons, some of them
painted in bright colors, had been left by the
side of the road. There were half a dozen
tents put up and several lines of clothes were
flapping lazily in the breeze.

"There are some gypsy children," Honey
Bunch whispered eagerly.

There were a good many gypsy children, in
fact, little ones and big. They tumbled on the
grass and when they saw Honey Bunch and
Stub they sat up and stared.

"They have on bracelets," whispered Honey
Bunch to Stub.

Not only the children, but the men and
women wore a good many bracelets and rings
and earrings. The bracelets had bangles and
clanked as the gypsies moved about. And they
wore the gayest clothes Honey Bunch had ever
seen—bright red and yellow waists and skirts
and flowered handkerchiefs around their
necks.

"Are they touring, too?" asked Honey
Bunch, as her mother gently turned her

around and began to stroll slowly back to their own camp.

Stub hung back a little, for she would have liked to stay longer. But she was not willing to be left alone, so when she found that her aunt and uncle were going on ahead, she ran after them and took Honey Bunch's hand again.

"The gypsies live in their wagons and tents all the time," Mr. Morton was explaining to Honey Bunch, when Stub caught up with her. "They move from place to place, because they like to live outdoors. For hundreds of years the gypsies have lived just like that."

"Why don't we?" asked Honey Bunch curiously.

"Why, Honey Bunch Morton, you wouldn't want to live in a wagon, or even an automobile, all the year round!" her mother exclaimed. "You'd miss our nice house and your flowers and Mrs. Miller and Norman Clark. And you wouldn't have any little girls to play with, like Ida Camp."

By the time they had reached their own tent,

Honey Bunch had decided that she didn't want to be a real gypsy.

"Just the same, sleeping outdoors in a tent is fun," giggled Stub, when they were safely tucked into their cots. "Say, Honey Bunch, suppose the car started off in the night and took the tent along with it! Just suppose!"

"Just suppose you go to sleep in there," Daddy Morton growled, pretending to be cross. "You're keeping Eleanor and Uncle Lysander awake."

The car did not start off in the night and Honey Bunch and Stub woke up to find themselves exactly where they had gone to sleep. Honey Bunch's daddy and mother were already up, and when Stub heard them talking, she was so eager to ask them if they were going to pass the gypsy camp on the way to her Great-Aunt Molly's that she jumped out of the cot, never noticed the blanket trailing behind her, and caught her foot in it just as she reached the tent door.

She stumbled and rolled out of the tent, almost to the feet of Honey Bunch's daddy, who picked her up and asked her if she was a breakfast roll.

"Oh, dear, I always catch my feet," mourned Stub. "Uncle David, are we going past the gypsy camp when we go to Great-Aunt Molly's?"

"I think so," he answered. "Who is going to the farmhouse for some milk for breakfast?"

Honey Bunch and Stub dressed quickly and went after the milk. They had a delicious breakfast of bacon and eggs cooked on the stove which fascinated Stub so much that Honey Bunch's mother had to watch her every minute to see that she did not stand too close to it. Then they packed the tent and the stove and put everything neatly in its place and began their journey again.

"There's a gypsy waving to us," said Honey Bunch, when they came in sight of the gypsy camp.

"It's a little girl gypsy," Stub added.

CHAPTER XII

AUTO CAMPING OUT

THE little girl gypsy had apparently never been told that children should keep out of the road, for she stood right in the center and calmly waited for the car to stop.

"Buy a bracelet?" she asked, when Mr. Morton brought the machine to a standstill. "Buy a bracelet for the little girl?"

"Well, I like that!" Stub cried indignantly. "I'm as big as she is."

"Have you two bracelets?" said Mr. Morton. "You see I have two little girls here."

The little girl gypsy flashed her white teeth in a swift smile and ducked back into the field. They saw her running to one of the tents, and in a few minutes she was back with another bracelet. They were made of colored beads strung together, and Honey Bunch and Stub thought they were beautiful.

Mr. Morton bought the two bracelets and the two little girls put them on at once. The gypsy girl stood and waved her scarlet sash— Honey Bunch insisted it was a sash, though she wore it wrapped around her head—until the car was out of sight.

"Now," said Stub, settling back and looking very important, "I have to begin to watch for Great-Aunt Molly's house."

They were still on the wrong road, but at the next crossroads Daddy Morton turned and the road map showed him that he was on the state highway where he wished to be. They stopped for lunch at a little country hotel and Stub, who had not traveled very much, would not let the waitress take her hat. She kept it on her lap all during the meal and it fell off three times and the waitress and a man at the table and Honey Bunch's daddy took turns picking it up. Stub was more interested in the waitress than she was in her food, and she whispered to Honey Bunch that she was never going to be a waitress.

"Just suppose I was carrying a tray of dishes

and I tripped," said Stub. "Think how dreadful that would be."

And Honey Bunch said no, she did not think that Stub should ever try to be a waitress when she grew up.

They found a little group of people around the car when they went out to resume their trip, and some one asked Mr. Morton if he was touring.

"There's a good state auto camp about forty miles on," said a man. "Most people going up to the Lakes make it a stopping place."

"We're going to spend the night there," Mr. Morton replied, while Honey Bunch and Stub scrambled into the car.

"I could go to Great-Aunt Molly's to-morrow morning," observed Stub, as they rolled smoothly down the road.

Honey Bunch's mother laughed and said that Great-Aunt Molly would be waiting.

"You know we'd love to have you with us, Stub," she said. "But your mother said to leave you at the house with the green blinds and the iron flower pots. And, dear me, it seems to me we are there this minute."

They were, too. Even if the green blinds and the iron flower pots had been missing, the little old lady who came down the gravel path between the two long flower beds would have told them that this was Great-Aunt Molly's house. The little old lady was Great-Aunt Molly herself.

She was very glad to see Stub and her shiny suitcase, and she urged the Mortons to spend the night with her. Stub looked as though she wanted them to stay very much, too— perhaps she was a little homesick at the idea of staying in a strange place without her mother—but Mr. Morton explained that he wanted to reach the auto camp that night.

A little curly poodle came running out of the house and jumped on Stub, and that made her feel better, so that when Honey Bunch looked back as the car drove away she saw her cousin hugging the dog with one hand and waving the arm that had the gypsy bracelet on it quite cheerfully to say good-bye.

"Stub wanted to see the auto camp," said Honey Bunch, who was now sitting between her mother and daddy, leaving Eleanor and Uncle Lysander alone on the back seat of the car.

"Perhaps next year we can take her touring with us," Daddy Morton answered. "And you can send her a postal from the camp."

Honey Bunch took a little nap that afternoon and the sun was setting when she opened her eyes and sat up. Great pink clouds filled the west and they seemed to be driving straight into them.

"Look at all the cars!" gasped Honey Bunch.

They were moving slowly, for they were in line. There were cars ahead of them and cars back of them, and before Honey Bunch could ask any questions they came to a huge gate that shut off a wide stretch of ground from the road. Behind this gate were dozens and dozens of automobiles and tents and stoves, like the one on Honey Bunch's daddy's car.

"It's the auto camp," said Honey Bunch.

And it was. They drove through the gate, under two huge painted signs, past a filling station and past parked cars till they came to a quiet corner near a tree. Mr. Morton stopped his car here, backed it in skillfully and smiled at Honey Bunch.

"Guess we'll have supper," he told her.

He got out the tent and put it up quickly and skillfully, while Honey Bunch's mother tied on her white apron and put the teakettle on the little stove. Honey Bunch knew where the dishes were, and she began to set the table. Mr. Morton said they were experienced campers and he was proud of them.

"Hello," said a little voice, as Honey Bunch came out of the tent to ask her mother where to find the paper napkins.

"Hello," Honey Bunch answered, a little shyly.

There stood a little girl about her own age, a boy a little older, and a baby in rompers, just old enough to walk.

"He's a boy," said the little girl as soon as

she saw Honey Bunch look at the baby.
"Every one always asks me. His hair is natu-
rally curly and folks think he is a girl. But
his name is Hiram."

Honey Bunch thought that Hiram wasn't
half as pretty a name as a baby with curly yellow hair and big blue eyes and two dimples
deserved, but she did not say so.

"Where are you going?" asked the older
boy. "We're going to Three Lakes."

Honey Bunch showed her pretty white
teeth in a quick smile.

"So are we," she informed him. "Are you
taking the Royal Green and Blue Tour?"

"No, we're going to spend Dad's vacation
up there," said the boy. "We've got a tent
just like yours and a stove and—"

"Billy! Billy!" called some one.

"That's Mother. We have to go to supper," said the boy. "Come out and play afterward, will you? Our car is the seventh from
the gate."

But after supper there were more cars
parked in the camp and there were so many

people walking about and so many children playing tag and running back and forth that Honey Bunch's mother thought she had better not go to the gate. Honey Bunch was sitting quietly, holding Eleanor and Uncle Lysander on her lap, when Billy and his sister came in search of her.

"Hiram's in bed," Billy said, when Honey Bunch asked for the baby. "Say, there are four girls in a closed car going to the lakes and two boys in the car back of ours. Lots of people are going this year."

The little girl, whose name, she said, was Sally, sat down beside Honey Bunch, and Billy sat down, too, and they began to get acquainted. By the time Honey Bunch had to go to bed she knew that Billy and Sally's last name was Bennett and that they lived in a town near New York, though they did not know her cousin, Julie, because she asked them and they said no. And Billy and Sally knew where Honey Bunch lived and how she had found Uncle Lysander and all about Lady Clare who was lost.

"Sally lost a cat once, but she thinks the ashman took it," said Honey Bunch as she was getting ready for bed. "The ashman didn't take Lady Clare."

"Perhaps when we get to the lakes we'll find a letter from Mrs. Miller, saying Lady Clare has come home," Mrs. Morton said hopefully.

The next morning every one in the camp was astir early. They were all going somewhere and they were anxious to start. Daddy Morton studied the road maps while he drank his coffee and Honey Bunch saw nothing of Billy or Sally or Hiram, though Sally had said she was coming before breakfast to show Honey Bunch a bracelet she had put away. Sally said it looked almost like Honey Bunch's gypsy bracelet.

"I think we'll take the longer route," said Daddy Morton when the tent was folded and everything packed and he was driving slowly out of the camp. "It will be less crowded and we are not in such a tearing hurry that six miles makes any great difference. Let's be comfortable as we go. Eh, Honey Bunch?"

"My, yes, Daddy," Honey Bunch replied seriously. "Mrs. Miller says give her her comfort every time—she doesn't believe in all this speeding."

Daddy Morton laughed and said he didn't believe in it either, and then he began to tell Honey Bunch one of her favorite stories about when he was a little boy. He had just reached the most exciting part when they heard some one shouting to them. A farmer, plowing in a field near the road, was calling.

"Hey, the bridge is broken down the road a piece," this farmer shouted. "You can't use it."

"Do we have to turn around?" Mr. Morton called back, while Honey Bunch and her mother listened anxiously.

"No—you can ford it. Guess you can make it all right," cried the farmer, and then he started his team again and went on with his plowing.

"This is our day for adventures," said Mr. Morton. "I haven't any idea how deep the water is, but rather than turn back, I think we'll try to ford it. We can put Honey Bunch on the roof of the car if the water comes in."

Honey Bunch thought it would be great fun to "ford" a stream, though she didn't know what that was. When her daddy stopped the car a few feet from the bridge, which was closed with two rails across it to warn motorists that it was unsafe, and began to take the tent and boxes from the running board, Honey Bunch was puzzled.

"The water will come up as high as that, if not higher," Daddy Morton explained. "There—I think we are all shipshape. Who wants to set sail with me?"

"We do," said Mrs. Morton, smiling. "Isn't this fun, Honey Bunch?"

Honey Bunch nodded, but she did not say anything, and when the car slid gently into the water she held Eleanor very tightly indeed. It seemed queer to be driving through the brook and, leaning over, she could see that the water was up to the running board.

"Oh—h," said Honey Bunch as, with a terrific snort and a burst of speed, the car shot up the bank on the other side. "Oh, Daddy, could we cross the New York river like that? Just like the ferryboats?"

"You mean the Hudson River?" Daddy Morton said quickly. "Well, no, Honey Bunch, I doubt if we could ford that; it is too deep. But little brooks we can attempt nicely. We don't miss the bridges at all, if the water isn't too deep."

But Honey Bunch was glad she was across the brook and she privately hoped that they would not have to ford any more streams. And they didn't because, after two or three more hours of driving, they coasted down a beautiful hill and there, at the bottom, spread out before them, were the three lakes—"The Triplets"—as smooth as glass and almost as blue as the sky they reflected.

"I wish I knew where we wanted to camp," said Mr. Morton, as he saw the tents and cottages and bungalows that dotted the shores of the lakes.

"I see just the place, Daddy," Honey Bunch

announced seriously. "I'd admire to camp in a place like that."

Mrs. Miller always said she would "admire" to do certain things, and Honey Bunch knew it meant she would be pleased.

"Where would you admire to camp, Miss Honey Bunch Morton?" asked her daddy.

Honey Bunch stood up and pointed. She thought her mother would forgive her this once—Mrs. Morton said it was most impolite to point—because it was so important.

"There, where those little white birch trees are, Daddy," said Honey Bunch. "On the other side of the middle lake."

"That is a pretty place," Mrs. Morton agreed. "Drive there, David, and we can see if it is a good spot for camping."

CHAPTER XIII

THE SPARE WHEEL

HONEY BUNCH'S daddy drove around the pretty winding road till they came to the group of four little white birch trees a short distance from the shore of the center lake.

"Why, it's lovely!" cried Mrs. Morton in delight. "Honey Bunch you have the brightest eyes of any little girl I know. We can camp here, can't we, David?"

"Don't see why not," Mr. Morton said pleasantly. "Guess there is nothing to do but set up the tent. Are we going to need things for supper, Edith?"

Mrs. Morton was reaching over the front seat of the car to get her apron which she had loaned Uncle Lysander as a pillow at Honey Bunch's suggestion.

"I think we have everything for to-night," she answered. "To-morrow I will give you

146

a list and you'll have to find out where we buy our supplies."

"Some one is waving to us," said Mr. Morton, in surprise. "Why, it is a child. Honey Bunch, do you know that little boy—or is it a girl?"

"It's Hiram!" Honey Bunch exclaimed. "You know Hiram Bennett, Daddy. And Billy and Sally must be around, too—they said they were coming to Three Lakes. Yes! Look over there! That's their car."

"Don't they ever call the baby anything else?" asked Mr. Morton. "Hiram seems such an—er—sad kind of name for a baby."

"Oh, Daddy, you couldn't call him anything else!" Honey Bunch protested. "That is his name."

But when Sally and Billy and Hiram came running up a few minutes later, it seemed that Hiram did have another name.

"Daddy calls him 'Snooks'," said Sally. "But I think nicknames are rather silly."

"Honey Bunch isn't a silly name," Billy declared. "That's a nickname. Say, Honey

Bunch, don't you want to go for the mail?
We're going."

"Where do you go?" asked Mrs. Morton,
who was beating eggs in a bowl as comfortably as though she were in her own home
kitchen.

"There's a post-office at the head of the first
lake," Billy explained. "It isn't more than
half a mile from here."

"Mail comes twice a day," added Sally.
"If you want any more than that you have to
go to Rushmore. That's where the stores
are."

"You must have been here before," Mr.
Morton told her smilingly. "Is Rushmore
where we buy our supplies—food and such
stuff?"

"You have to buy everything there," Sally
informed him. "Mr. Moffatt, the man who
owns the lakes, won't have any stores on his
land. This is the first year they have had a
post-office. We have been coming here for
five years," she finished.

Honey Bunch's daddy said if his little girl

was not too tired she might walk to the post-office with Billy and Sally.

"Ask for letters for Mr. and Mrs. David Morton and Miss Honey Bunch Morton," he directed her.

"Come round by our car a minute. We have to leave Hiram, for he can't walk as far as that," said Sally.

Sally's mother was short and fat and she had the most cheerful smile. She reminded Honey Bunch a little of Mrs. Miller, for when she laughed she shook all over and her face turned red. She said she had heard all about Honey Bunch and she hoped she would like Three Lakes.

Honey Bunch and Sally and Billy set off for the post-office, and Honey Bunch saw much to interest her on the way. There were a great many cars with tents and camping out-fits like Daddy Morton's, and there were little cottages that looked like dolls' playhouses. There were wharves and boats tied to them and a dozen or so boats being rowed about the lakes.

"I like it here," said Honey Bunch happily.

"Of course you do! It is a nice place," Billy told her gravely. "Here is the post-office. Be sure you ask for the mail the way your father told you."

Billy was so determined that Honey Bunch should not forget, that he stood right at her elbow while she raised herself on her tiptoes and held on to the window sill with both hands.

"If you please," said Honey Bunch clearly, "is there any mail for Mr. David Morton or Mrs. Morton or Miss Honey Bunch Morton?"

The clerk wore glasses and he peered down at her as if he could hardly see her.

"I'll look," he said.

And, my goodness, didn't he hand out letters for every one—even for Honey Bunch, who didn't expect a letter and was so surprised she almost dropped it on the floor. There were letters and two newspapers and a maga-

zine and, yes, a picture postal card—this for
Honey Bunch, too.

"You got a lot of mail," said Billy respect-
fully. "I suppose you told folks you were
coming here and they sent letters on ahead.
That is the way we do when my Aunt Chris-
tine travels in Europe—we send her letters
ahead and some times she never gets them."

Honey Bunch felt very proud of the mail
she carried, and when she showed it all to her
daddy and mother they were surprised, too.
Nothing was opened till after supper, and
then Honey Bunch's daddy said she should
read her mail first because she would be the
first one to have to go to bed.

The card was from Stub who, she wrote,
was having a "perfectly lovely time" visiting
her Great-Aunt Molly. She had two kinds of
dessert every day.

The letter was from Mrs. Miller, and, alas,
Mrs. Miller wrote to say that Lady Clare had
not come home.

"I go to the house every day," wrote the

kind washerwoman, "and I put clean sweet
milk in the saucer and leave a bit of something
nice on the plate. But no sign of Lady Clare
have I seen. Mrs. Farriday and Mrs. Perkins are both watching for her, and the moment they see her they will take her indoors,
so she can not run away. But I think you'll
be glad to know, Honey Bunch, that some
poor hungry cats whose families have gone
away and left them with nothing to eat sometimes come and drink Lady Clare's milk—so
it does some cat a world of good, you see."

Honey Bunch was glad that a hungry cat
should drink the milk, but she cried a little
when she was in bed that night. She loved
Lady Clare dearly and she was sure that the
kitty could not be happy roaming the streets
of Barham, if that was what she was doing.
Lady Clare was not used to roaming. She
had always had a cushion of her own and a
back fence she had to share with no one except Norman, and he did not bother her very
often.

In a few days Honey Bunch felt as though

she had spent weeks at the Three Lakes. She
made friends with a number of children and
they went bathing together and walked around
the lakes and tried to fish, though they did
not have any luck at all. Whenever some one
went to Rushmore for supplies—which was
pretty nearly every day—any boy or girl who
happened to be near was invited to go along.
At home some of them grumbled if they were
asked to go to the store for their mothers, but
this going in an automobile, they said, was different. Besides, the stores in town were filled
with fascinating things and you could see anything from a rowboat to a five-bulb radio set.

Several families had brought their radio
sets with them, and Honey Bunch often went
to sleep at night listening to the music. She
didn't mind going to bed early—earlier even
than Hiram, who had a bad habit of staying
up as late as he could coax his mother to let
him—because sleeping in the tent was such
fun.

"Honey Bunch, you take to camping as a
duck does to water," her daddy told her.

And Honey Bunch, sunburned and busy and happy, said she was having "just the nicest time."

One afternoon, after they had been at the camp almost two weeks, Mrs. Morton said she thought that she and Honey Bunch deserved a little treat.

"We managed to bake a pie yesterday and had a great time keeping the oven where it belonged," she explained. "So, it seems to me that two such good cooks ought to be rewarded."

"I think so, too. That was a fine pie," said Mr. Morton heartily. "What do you suggest?"

"Ice-cream," said Honey Bunch.

"A little drive," Mrs. Morton added. "We can go through Rushmore and explore that hill road you hear so much about. Honey Bunch can have her cream when we go through the town."

They started as soon as lunch was over and by the time they had bought several things in Rushmore that they needed for camp, Honey

Bunch's daddy said he supposed she was hungry enough to eat ice-cream if lunch *had* been only an hour ago. Honey Bunch was sure she was hungry enough, so they went to the drug store and Honey Bunch had vanilla and her mother had strawberry and her daddy had chocolate. And very good it was indeed.

"If that hill road is too bad, don't try it, David," said Mrs. Morton when they were once more settled in the car. "We can stay on the main road and see where that goes."

"I'd like to go round the Robber's Nose," said Daddy Morton, with a smile for Honey Bunch.

"A real robber's nose, Daddy?" asked that small girl eagerly.

"No—a make-believe one," he told her. "It is a hill that people with imagination say looks like a man's nose. We'll see for ourselves."

The hill road turned off abruptly from the main highway and it was narrow and rather rocky. But beautiful trees lined it on either side and when they had climbed a steep hill they could see for miles. Mr. Morton stopped the car and Honey Bunch looked back and saw the lakes and the tents and the cottages, which looked like little dots.

"Mercy, look at the hill we have to go down," said Mrs. Morton, when they went on.

"It's a gradual slope," her husband pointed out. "We'll not find it as steep as it looks from here."

The road was rough and Honey Bunch was afraid that Eleanor would be uncomfortable. The doll and Uncle Lysander were on the back seat—everywhere that Honey Bunch went, these two faithful friends went, too— and she was watching anxiously to see that Eleanor did not tumble to the floor when Bang! a loud report like a pistol startled her.

"Oh, dear!" Mrs. Morton looked distressed. "A blowout!"

Honey Bunch's daddy pulled the car to one side of the road and stopped.

"'Fraid so," he said good-temperedly.

SHE STARTED AFTER THE WHEEL.

Honey Bunch : Her First Auto Tour.

Page 151

"And I came off without the jack—loaned it
to Bennett last night."

Honey Bunch remembered that Sally and
Billy's father had come over after she was in
bed and asked for something. Now he had
no jack which they needed to raise the wheel
from the road and hold it up while a new tire
was put on.

"Some one in a car will come along and
help us out," said Mr. Morton cheerfully,
"and meanwhile I might as well get the spare
wheel ready."

Strapped on the back of the car was an
extra wheel which could be put on in less time
than a tire. Mr. Morton unstrapped this and
rolled it around to the front of the car—one
of the front tires had blown out—and left it
leaning against the hood.

"Edith, I wish you'd come back and look
at the trunk straps while you have a chance,"
he said to Honey Bunch's mother. "One looks
as though it ought to be replaced."

Mrs. Morton followed him around to the
back of the car and Honey Bunch strayed to

the front wheel, intending to look at the blow-out which was causing them all this trouble.

"I wonder if a spare wheel is heavy?" she thought to herself.

She grasped the spare wheel and made it stand upright, but it was a clumsy thing to hold and her little hands slipped. Away rolled that wheel, for all the world like a hoop, spinning down the hill.

"Oh, my!" exclaimed Honey Bunch, in great dismay.

Then she started after the wheel.

CHAPTER XIV

THROUGH THE WOODS

THE wheel rolled faster and faster. If Honey Bunch had had time, she would have liked to stop and watch it, because no hoop of hers had ever rolled so beautifully. But she had no time to stop, for she had to catch the wheel.

"I hope it doesn't bounce off," thought Honey Bunch anxiously, trying to run faster yet. "If it bounces off, I never could find it."

Honey Bunch was running so fast now that she could not have stopped if she had wished to. She struck a stone and almost fell down —she was reminded of her cousin Stub, who usually did fall down—but she kept her balance and went on down the hill.

Then, when the bottom of the hill was almost reached, the wheel did just what she hoped it would not do.

It bounced off!

"Now you're lost!" scolded the nearly breathless Honey Bunch. "Oh, dear, wouldn't it be awful if I couldn't find you?"

But she remembered where the wheel had left the road, and when she reached that place, she turned off, too. The wheel had rolled into the woods, and very cool and shady it was under the trees after that long hot run down the hill. Honey Bunch drew a long breath of pleasure.

"Isn't it nice?" she said aloud, and a little chipmunk in a tree over her head chattered a polite answer.

"I don't see where that wheel went," said Honey Bunch, who liked to talk to herself, "but I must find it for my daddy. This is a path and the wheel must have rolled right down here."

Honey Bunch was so interested in looking for the wheel that she did not feel lonely, though she was a very little girl alone in a strange woods. She trudged along the narrow path and every time she came to an unusually

large tree she walked around it, to see if the
wheel had "bounced off" again and rolled
around a tree and hidden. But there was no
wheel anywhere to be found.

"I am kind of thirsty," Honey Bunch said
presently. "I wish I had a chocolate soda
with strawberry ice-cream."

But that only made her thirstier, so she
stopped thinking about it.

"Anyway, my mother says vanilla ice-cream
is better for you," she told a gray squirrel, who
was frisking along the path just ahead of her.

The squirrel wasn't interested in ice-cream
and he darted off, intent on his own affairs.
Then Honey Bunch felt lonely for the first
time.

"I don't see where that wheel could have
gone," she said slowly. "I've looked everywhere. And I wish I had a drink of water
and it feels like a stone in my shoe and perhaps I'd better go back and tell Daddy the
wheel is lost."

She sat down on the ground and took off
her shoe—there was a little flat pebble in it.

The woods were so still and the air was so cool, though there was no breeze and not a leaf on the trees stirred, that Honey Bunch rather wished to lie down and take a little nap. But she remembered her mother and daddy would be waiting for her.

She put on her shoe and started back. But, though she was careful to walk in the exact direction she had taken in coming, she seemed to be walking deeper and deeper into the woods. In fact, she couldn't find the road at all!

"I should have brought Norman's compass," she said anxiously. "I could tip it and find the north."

By this time she had forgotten all about the wheel, and all she wanted was to find her way back to the car. She began to run, tripping over roots and stones half covered with moss. Something bounced out of the bushes ahead of her as she was running, and poor Honey Bunch cried, "Daddy! Daddy!" though there was no one to hear her.

But she saw in another minute that it was a

rabbit that had frightened her—a young rabbit, hardly "grown up at all," as she told Mrs. Miller long afterward. The rabbit was as much frightened as Honey Bunch was and his little heart was beating as fast as hers. His eyes, too, as he galloped ahead of her, were wide with fear.

"He thinks I'm chasing him," said Honey Bunch softly.

So she stopped and the rabbit bounded on and no doubt told his mother at supper that night of the narrow escape he had had when a great big girl chased him in the woods and almost caught him.

Honey Bunch walked more slowly after that, partly so she might not frighten any more rabbits and partly because she was very tired. Her feet made no sound on the soft earth, and when she came around a large briary bush, she walked straight into a boy who had not heard her coming.

Honey Bunch had not heard him, either, and they were both surprised. The boy was more surprised than Honey Bunch, because

she thought anything might happen in the
woods and he had walked through them a hun-
dred times and never seen a little girl like
Honey Bunch.

"Gee whiz!" said the boy, who reminded
Honey Bunch of Ned Camp.

Ned was Ida's big brother and he went to
high school and he was a very nice boy indeed
and hardly ever teased his little sister or her
friends.

"Where did you come from?" asked the
boy. "Airplane drop you out of the skies?"

"I came in an automobile," Honey Bunch
answered politely.

The boy stared around and she hurried to
explain.

"It's 'way off there—somewhere," she said,
pointing through the trees. "I was chasing
the spare wheel and I got lost."

"I should think you were lost," the boy answered. "I don't know what road you mean,
but there are four state roads which border
this woods. Where is this spare wheel you
were chasing?"

"It rolled into the woods and I was hunting for it," said Honey Bunch earnestly. "You didn't see it, did you?"

The boy shook his head.

"No, I didn't see it," he replied. "I came out to the spring to get a bucket of water for Grandma. She won't drink the well water in summer—says it isn't cold enough."

Then Honey Bunch noticed for the first time that he had a bucket on his arm.

"Please could I have a drink?" she asked. "I'm so thirsty."

"Why, you poor little tyke, you look worn out," said the boy. "Of course you shall have a drink. Wait a minute and I'll make you a leaf cup."

In less than a minute he had a leaf pinned together with the long briars and filled with cold water for Honey Bunch. She drank three leaf cups full, and never had she tasted anything so good as that cold, cold spring water.

"I'll have to take you home with me," said the boy, when she had had enough. "You're

lost and your people will be having fits. My
name is Fred and my grandmother will know
what to do with you."

Honey Bunch slipped her hand into Fred's
and smiled at him.

"I could help you carry the bucket," she
suggested.

"No, I can manage it," Fred said. "We
haven't far to go. I could carry you, only
I have this pesky bucket."

Honey Bunch didn't see where any one
could live in the woods, but she found out in
a few moments that Fred did not live in the
woods. The path led them to an open place
and there was a little brown and white house
and a barn and a flock of white chickens running about the yard.

"There's Grandma feeding the chickens,"
said Fred.

A tall thin woman with white hair held a
pan and was scattering grain from it for the
chickens who pushed and scrambled at her
feet.

"Why, Fred, whose little girl is that?" the

white-haired woman called when she looked
up and saw Honey Bunch and Fred coming
toward the house.

"I found her in the woods," answered Fred,
for by this time they had reached the yard.
"But I forgot to ask her her name."

Fred's grandmother smiled at Honey Bunch
and lifted her up to sit on the high, square
gate-post.

"Whose little girl are you?" she asked cheerfully.

"I am Daddy's girl," Honey Bunch replied.
"I'm Honey Bunch Morton and I was chasing the spare wheel and it rolled away and
hid in the woods."

"But how do we let Daddy know where
you are?" the grandmother asked. "He will
be so worried. I know he would much rather
lose a spare wheel than a little girl. No one
ever has a little girl to spare."

Honey Bunch looked troubled.

"She left them in an automobile on the
road," said Fred.

But as soon as his grandmother heard that

the Mortons were camping at the Three Lakes she said she knew what to do.

"Fred, you'll have to go to Leland's and telephone to the post-office at the Lakes," she said. "You can't hope to find the road to-night, and some one at the post-office will be sure to know how to get in touch with Honey Bunch's people. Hurry like a good boy and I'll have supper ready when you come back."

Fred hurried away—there was no telephone ın the little brown and white house and he had to walk two miles to reach one—and Honey Bunch and Fred's grandmother went into the kitchen.

Honey Bunch was tired, she was sleepy, but she wanted to help.

"I know how to set the table," she said bravely, "and I can push the chairs up for you."

"Dearie, you sit down in this nice big rocking chair and hold Simple Simon for me," said Fred's grandmother. "You don't know my name, do you? I am Grandma Cory, and here is my cat."

There in the rocking chair, close to the stove, was a big gray cat. This was Simple Simon, and Honey Bunch began to feel at home as soon as she had him on her lap. While Grandma Cory cooked supper, she told her about Lady Clare and Fred's grandma said that she was sure Lady Clare would come back.

"Cats are great homebodies," said Grandma. "My, yes, you can hardly drag a cat away from its home. As soon as Lady Clare knows you are home again, I wouldn't be a bit surprised if she came marching straight back."

This was comforting to hear, and when Fred came in and said that he had telephoned the post-office and the postmaster had promised to send a boy on a bicycle to find Mr. Morton wherever he was and deliver the message that Honey Bunch was safe and well, she was ready to be interested in supper.

But before she had finished her toast and strawberry jam and milk and rice, poor little Honey Bunch was so sleepy she couldn't keep her eyes open. You see she had walked a long distance, and that made her tired. She hardly knew when Fred carried her into bed and she didn't even miss her own dear mother, for she was sound asleep before Grandma Cory had undressed her and covered her with a pretty gray blanket.

She was very much surprised to wake up in the morning and find herself in a tiny little room instead of in her cot in the tent. The door of the room was open and she saw Grandma Cory moving around, getting breakfast. And suddenly it seemed to Honey Bunch that she just must see her mother!

She jumped out of bed and ran to the door.

"I would like to go home, please," she said gravely.

Grandma Cory turned and smiled at her very sweetly.

"So you shall, dearie," she promised. "Just the minute you are dressed and have your breakfast, Fred will take you home. I'll come and help you right away."

Honey Bunch was dressed and had eaten her breakfast in less than half an hour. She was very eager to start, but she remembered how good Grandma had been to her.

"I've had a very nice time," she said, putting her arms around Grandma Cory and giving her a hug and a kiss, "and I hope you will come and see us soon."

Grandma Cory chuckled a little and kissed Honey Bunch twice, patting her on the back as she did so.

"You tell your mother I am sorry for all the worry I know she has had, but that she is luckier than Grandma Cory, for she has a little girl and I have none," she said softly.

"Fred is nice," Honey Bunch declared. "You have him."

She put her hand in Fred's and they began their walk through the woods.

CHAPTER XV

HOME AGAIN

"YOU know we can't walk all the way," said Fred, as Honey Bunch tried to take as long steps as he did.

"Why can't we?" she asked.

"Too far," Fred answered. "We'll cut through to the Mossville road and take a bus. That goes to Triplet Lakes."

Honey Bunch was so glad she was going to see her daddy and mother that she couldn't walk slowly. She hopped and skipped and hummed little tunes and she wasn't a bit afraid of losing her way this time. Not with Fred. He knew just where all the paths in the woods went. He said so.

"I've lived here all my life," he told her. "Now, if you hear a noise like thunder, that means a bus is coming and we'll have to run.

They are an hour apart, so we don't want to miss one."

They had almost reached the road when Honey Bunch heard a noise.

"Thunder!" she screamed. "Thunder! The bus is coming!" and she began to run as fast as she could.

Fred laughed, but he caught up with her and took her hand. Together they raced for the road, and as they stepped out from the trees a wide yellow bus lumbered up and stopped.

"Two passengers, eh?" said the driver, as Fred lifted Honey Bunch up the high step. "Through to the Lakes?"

"Through to the Lakes," Fred replied, and he helped Honey Bunch climb up on the slippery leather seat.

There were only two or three other passengers in the bus, and these got off before they reached Three Lakes. Honey Bunch was so interested in watching the driver drive that she did not notice when the car swung around and stopped in front of the post-office. But the postmaster saw her and came running out.

"Your folks are looking for you," he said to Honey Bunch. "Your mother never slept a wink last night, though I told her you were all right and coming home this morning."

"Where will I find her father and mother?" Fred asked quickly.

"I'll run you over to their camp in my car," said the postmaster. "That's the best plan."

He bundled Honey Bunch and Fred into his rusty little car and set off at top speed for the birch trees where the Mortons were camping.

All the campers had heard that Honey Bunch was lost and that some one had telephoned she was found and that she was expected back this morning. As the postmaster's car sped along the road, people saw Honey Bunch sitting in Fred's lap and they called and waved to her.

"She's found! The little lost girl is found!" the campers called joyously, and the word spread from cottage to bungalow and from bungalow to the automobiles.

Mrs. Morton heard the car coming and she ran out to meet it.

"My darling!" she was saying over and over. "My darling little Honey Bunch! Daddy, Daddy, come quickly! Honey Bunch is home!"

Well, Honey Bunch cried a little—because she was *so* glad to see her mother—and her mother cried a little, too—because she was *so* glad to see Honey Bunch—and Daddy Morton laughed at them both. But he hugged Honey Bunch so hard he hurt her and she knew he was glad to see her.

Then Honey Bunch told how she had chased the wheel and how she found herself in the woods and Fred told how he had met her walking down the wood trail and how he had taken her home to spend the night with his grandmother. Fred wanted to get back to the brown and white house, for he had work to do, and Daddy Morton said he would take him in the car. Honey Bunch and her mother stayed at the camping place and while her daddy was away, Honey Bunch heard how

her mother had missed her when she called to
her to come and hold a monkey wrench for
her daddy.

"I thought you didn't hear me when you
didn't answer," explained Honey Bunch's
mother, "and I went around to the side of the
car to call you again. And there, far down
the road, I saw a little black speck running
very fast! I called Daddy and he said it must
be you, but we didn't know what could make
you run off like that.

"Daddy started to run after you and I
stopped a car that came by a few minutes
later, but by the time we got down the hill,
you had disappeared. We hunted and hunted
and stopped every car to ask if they had seen
a little girl anywhere. Then Daddy borrowed
a jack and got the tire fixed so he could use
it and we rode up and down, calling for you.
At last a boy on a bicycle came rushing down
the hill and told us that some one had telephoned the postmaster that you were safe in
a farmhouse and that the people would bring

you home in the morning. Then we found the
lost wheel and went home, and Mother
thought all night long of her little girl."

Honey Bunch patted her mother's cheek
softly.

"Didn't you know I was chasing the spare
wheel, Mother?" she asked.

Mrs. Morton sighed a little.

"Daddy and I didn't give much thought to
the spare wheel while our little girl was lost,"
she admitted. "We were so anxious there
wasn't room in our minds for that."

Mr. Morton came back in an hour or so
and nothing would do but Honey Bunch and
her mother must go for a picnic with him.
They invited Billy and Sally and Hiram, and
no one had to pack any lunch, for Mr. Morton said it was to be his party. They went
to a hotel several miles away and had a chicken
dinner. Hiram was not used to eating dinner
away from home, but he behaved beautifully,
and when he grew a little tired, waiting for
the dessert to come, Honey Bunch showed

him the compass Norman had given her and he was so interested in that that he forgot to fret.

There were not many days left before the Mortons were to start for home. They wanted to make the trip by easy stages and Honey Bunch had set her heart on going to see Mr. and Mrs. Popover. It seemed that all the friends they had made at Three Lakes were determined to do something nice for Honey Bunch before she went home. She went to a party in one tent. A little girl at one of the cottages asked her to come and spend the night with her, but Honey Bunch's mother didn't want her to spend another night away from home, so Honey Bunch had supper with the little girl and her daddy came and got her at bedtime.

The day before they were going home there was a large marshmallow roast down by the center lake, and Honey Bunch and Sally and Billy—Hiram had to stay at home because his mother was afraid he would fall in the lake— roasted marshmallows on long pointed sticks

that Honey Bunch's daddy sharpened for
them.

Then, bright and early the next morning,
they packed everything into the car, said good-
bye to the friendly campers, and rolled
smoothly and silently down the road, past the
post-office, where the postmaster came out and
shook hands with them and said he hoped
they would come back next summer, out to
the main highway.

"We're going home!" sang Honey Bunch to
Uncle Lysander and Eleanor. "We're going
home and I like to go home. I want to see
Ida Camp and Norman Clark and Mrs. Miller. And maybe—Lady Clare."

But the last letter from Mrs. Miller had
told Honey Bunch's mother that the cat was
still missing. Yet, Honey Bunch thought
hopefully, she might come home when she
heard that her little mistress was back.

They reached Mr. and Mrs. Popover's
house late that afternoon, and the old man and
his wife would not let them go on. They insisted they must spend the night and they

made such a fuss over Honey Bunch that her
daddy said he must keep an eye on her or
Mrs. Popover might hide her in her work-
basket and try to keep her.

All the cats that Honey Bunch remembered
—Emerald and Ruby and Pearl—were grown
up, but there was a basket of new kittens, and
Mrs. Popover, when she heard that Lady
Clare was lost, wanted Honey Bunch to take
one home with her.

"But I would rather not, Mother," Honey
Bunch confided, when she went to bed that
night in the old-fashioned four-posted bed that
almost filled Mrs. Popover's guest room. "I
wouldn't want Lady Clare to think another
cat could make me forget her."

Of course when Mrs. Popover heard that
she understood at once and said that she was
afraid she had forgotten Lady Clare's feelings.

They had popovers for breakfast, and very
good they were, and as soon as the pleasant
meal was over Daddy Morton said it was time
to start, for he must get home that same day.

Mr. and Mrs. Popover came out to the car to see their guests off, and the lunch box they put in made Mrs. Morton laugh when she opened it at noon—there was food enough in it, she said, for a hungry army.

"Good-bye, Honey Bunch!" called the old man and the little old lady, as the car rolled away. "Good-bye, dear little Honey Bunch. Come to see us again."

"Now," said Honey Bunch, as she settled back in her place, "wouldn't it be nice if we could see Ruth Evans—just a minute."

Though her daddy and mother laughed at her, sure enough, Honey Bunch did see the little girl she had seen only once before and yet remembered so plainly.

Ruth remembered Honey Bunch, too. She was down at the mail box and had just raised the lid when the big shiny car drove up close to her and a little girl began to shout:

"Hello, Ruth Evans. Hello, Ruth Evans. I'm glad to see you!"

"Why, it's Honey Bunch!" cried Ruth, in great surprise. "Why, it's Honey Bunch

Morton! I got your note! Did you see your
Cousin Stub?"

Honey Bunch said yes, and then she explained that she had been to see Stub and she
told Ruth about the automobile tour and
showed her the tent and the camping equip-
ment and told her about Three Lakes.

"I don't suppose you'd have time to come
and see me, would you?" asked Ruth eagerly.

"We have to drive straight home, Ruth,"
Mrs. Morton said kindly. "But we are so
glad to have seen you. Honey Bunch has told
all her friends in Barham about you, and I
know she thinks of you often."

Then Honey Bunch kissed Ruth and Ruth
kissed Honey Bunch. They took just one
more extra minute to look at Uncle Lysander
and Eleanor and then the car started and the
Mortons were really going, as Honey Bunch
said, "straight home."

You know how pleasant it is to go away and
that it is even more pleasant to come home.
As soon as the car struck the familiar road
that led into Barham, Honey Bunch began to

watch for familiar landmarks. When they
finally rolled into their home city and she saw
the butcher where Mrs. Morton went market-
ing and the candy store and then, at last, their
very own Grove Street, she felt like singing.

"I hope Mrs. Miller has the house aired
and the windows open," said Honey Bunch's
mother. "I wrote to her to stay and get dinner for us to-night. But she may not have
received the letter."

Norman Clark was on the sidewalk and he
saw the car and recognized it.

"Honey Bunch is coming back!" he began
to shout. "Honey Bunch is coming back!
Say, Honey Bunch, there are only two counters left in your chicken game. I lost all the
others, Honey Bunch."

But Honey Bunch paid no attention to him.
Before the car stopped she had seen something
that made her forget all about games. There,
lying on the top step of the Morton house,
four furry paws neatly folded under her, was
a beautiful black cat with a white ermine collar around her neck.

"Lady Clare!" Honey Bunch cried. "My darling Lady Clare! Daddy, Lady Clare has come home!"

So she had, and in another minute Mrs. Miller was hugging Honey Bunch and Honey Bunch was hugging her cat. Mrs. Miller said she had not seen Lady Clare till that moment, so the cat must have been waiting for her little mistress to come back. Honey Bunch was sure that was the way it was, and certainly Lady Clare never contradicted her. She was glad to be at home, and Honey Bunch was, too, so we may leave them both quite happily.

THE END

THE HONEY BUNCH BOOKS

By HELEN LOUISE THORNDYKE

Individual Colored Wrappers and Text Illustrations

Honey Bunch is a dainty, thoughtful little girl, and to know her is to take her to your heart at once.

Little girls everywhere will want to discover what interesting experiences she is having wherever she goes.

HONEY BUNCH: JUST A LITTLE GIRL
HONEY BUNCH: HER FIRST VISIT TO THE CITY
HONEY BUNCH: HER FIRST DAYS ON THE FARM
HONEY BUNCH: HER FIRST VISIT TO THE SEASHORE
HONEY BUNCH: HER FIRST LITTLE GARDEN
HONEY BUNCH: HER FIRST DAYS IN CAMP
HONEY BUNCH: HER FIRST AUTO TOUR
HONEY BUNCH: HER FIRST TRIP ON THE OCEAN
HONEY BUNCH: HER FIRST TRIP WEST
HONEY BUNCH: HER FIRST SUMMER ON AN ISLAND
HONEY BUNCH: HER FIRST TRIP ON THE GREAT LAKES
HONEY BUNCH: HER FIRST TRIP IN AN AEROPLANE
HONEY BUNCH: HER FIRST VISIT TO THE ZOO
HONEY BUNCH: HER FIRST BIG ADVENTURE
HONEY BUNCH: HER FIRST BIG PARADE
HONEY BUNCH: HER FIRST LITTLE MYSTERY

GROSSET & DUNLAP :-: *Publishers* :-: NEW YORK

THE BOBBSEY TWINS BOOKS
FOR LITTLE MEN AND WOMEN
By LAURA LEE HOPE

ILLUSTRATED. *Every volume complete in itself.*

These books for boys and girls between the ages of three and ten stand among children and their parents of this generation where the books of Louisa May Alcott stood in former days. The haps and mishaps of this inimitable pair of twins, their many adventures and experiences are a source of keen delight to imaginative children.

THE BOBBSEY TWINS
THE BOBBSEY TWINS IN THE COUNTRY
THE BOBBSEY TWINS AT THE SEASHORE
THE BOBBSEY TWINS AT SCHOOL
THE BOBBSEY TWINS AT SNOW LODGE
THE BOBBSEY TWINS ON A HOUSEBOAT
THE BOBBSEY TWINS AT MEADOW BROOK
THE BOBBSEY TWINS AT HOME
THE BOBBSEY TWINS IN A GREAT CITY
THE BOBBSEY TWINS ON BLUEBERRY ISLAND
THE BOBBSEY TWINS ON THE DEEP BLUE SEA
THE BOBBSEY TWINS IN WASHINGTON
THE BOBBSEY TWINS IN THE GREAT WEST
THE BOBBSEY TWINS AT CEDAR CAMP
THE BOBBSEY TWINS AT THE COUNTY FAIR
THE BOBBSEY TWINS CAMPING OUT
THE BOBBSEY TWINS AND BABY MAY
THE BOBBSEY TWINS KEEPING HOUSE
THE BOBBSEY TWINS AT CLOVERBANK
THE BOBBSEY TWINS AT CHERRY CORNER
THE BOBBSEY TWINS AND THEIR SCHOOLMATES
THE BOBBSEY TWINS TREASURE HUNTING
THE BOBBSEY TWINS AT SPRUCE LAKE
THE BOBBSEY TWINS WONDERFUL SECRET
THE BOBBSEY TWINS AT THE CIRCUS
THE BOBBSEY TWINS ON AN AIRPLANE TRIP
THE BOBBSEY TWINS SOLVE A MYSTERY
THE BOBBSEY TWINS ON A RANCH
THE BOBBSEY TWINS IN ESKIMO LAND

GROSSET & DUNLAP :-: *Publishers* :-: NEW YORK

Three Stories of Fun and Friendship

THE MAIDA BOOKS
by INEZ HAYNES IRWIN

MAIDA'S LITTLE SHOP

In a darling little shop of her own Maida makes many friends with the school children who buy her fascinating wares.

MAIDA'S LITTLE HOUSE

All of her friends spend a happy summer in Maida's perfect little house that has everything a child could wish for.

MAIDA'S LITTLE SCHOOL

Three delightful grownups come to visit and the children study many subjects without knowing that they are really "going to school."

GROSSET & DUNLAP   *Publishers*   NEW YORK

The Little Indian Series
By DAVID CORY

The beauty of Indian legend—the thrill of Indian adventure—the poetry of the Indian's religion, and, above all, perhaps, the sturdy manhood and the idealism of the Indian boy will be an inspiration to every child.

LITTLE INDIAN

The life of Little Indian, on the prairie and in the forest, is full of exciting adventures. His battle with the wildcat that, in the dead of night, attacks his favorite pony; his escape from a band of hostile Indians to the island of the Great Beaver; his pursuit of the red-winged goose and her seven snow-white goslings will thrill and stir the young imagination.

RED FEATHER

"Red Feather" is the warrior name given to "Little Indian." In this story the boy learns some of the secrets of healing and his friends, the animals, teach him the Medicine Song. He goes out on his first big hunt with the braves of the tribe and through his daring and skill wins his war shield. And now, no longer considered a child, he is sent on his first important mission for the tribe.

WHITE OTTER

Red Feather has won the admiration and friendship of everyone but the jealous and cowardly boy, White Otter. This mean-spirited youth seeks every opportunity to harm the son of Big Chief. Thus when Red Feather is sent on an important mission to Three Feathers, chief of a friendly tribe, White Otter follows him. But his plot to harm and disgrace Red Feather fails and the son of Big Chief safely reaches the distant camp.

STAR MAIDEN

Now Red Feather, first known as "Little Indian", has grown to manhood and has proved himself a worthy son of his father Big Chief. But he has to prove himself still further before he wins the heart and hand of lovely Star Maiden. For many moons he strives and at last he brings her to his father's camp where she is welcomed as his bride.

GROSSET & DUNLAP   *Publishers*   NEW YORK